ALSO BY ELIZABETH BERG

We Are All Welcome Here
The Year of Pleasures
The Art of Mending
Say When
True to Form
Ordinary Life: Stories
Never Change
Open House
Escaping into the Open: The Art of Writing True
Until the Real Thing Comes Along
What We Keep
Joy School
The Pull of the Moon
Range of Motion
Talk Before Sleep
Durable Goods
Family Traditions

THE HANDMAID
and
THE CARPENTER

DOUBLEDAY LARGE PRINT HOME LIBRARY EDITION

RANDOM HOUSE | NEW YORK

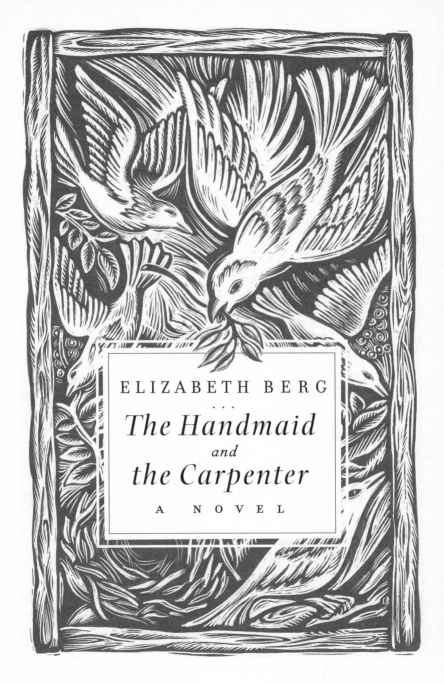

ELIZABETH BERG

· · ·

The Handmaid
and
the Carpenter

A NOVEL

This Large Print Edition, prepared especially for Doubleday Large Print Home Library, contains the complete, unabridged text of the original Publisher's Edition.

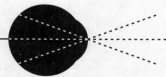

This Large Print Book carries the Seal of Approval of N.A.V.H.

To Marion Jeanne Hoff

And Nathanael said unto Philip,

Can there any good thing come out of Nazareth?

. . .

—*John 1:46*

The Bible is poetry. As such, it is open to interpretation. Here is one more writer's imagining of events that took place long, long ago. I have taken great license with the varying and often contradictory "facts" about Mary, Joseph, and the birth of Jesus; but then, I am in good company in doing so.

A word about dates. In this novel, Jesus is born in 4 B.C. That is because Matthew and Luke place Jesus' birth at the end of the reign of Herod the Great, who died in 4 B.C.

THE HANDMAID

and

THE CARPENTER

PROLOGUE

. . .

Nazareth, province of Galilee, Palestine
SEPTEMBER A.D. 9

Joseph

Overhead, above the flat roof he lies on, the moon is full and patient-seeming. Thin black clouds drift across it like floating veils. He can make out the silvery olive trees near the house, the gentle rise of hills behind them, even the high walls of limestone beyond that. The long grasses move in the night wind, and he strains to hear better the faint sound of some animal he cannot identify. His back pains him and he cries out, shifting one shoulder reflexively. The movement causes him to draw in a sharp breath; he holds it, then lets it slowly leave his body. Better. This is the way, to release without protest. He hears someone coming and struggles to sit up. One of his sons? No. It is his wife, when he wanted so for her not to know he had left her side. His cry must have awakened her, and now she has come to him in haste, barefoot and sleep-tousled, a shawl wrapped carelessly about her.

She sits beside him. "Why are you come here again?" She runs her hand, so light and cool, across his brow. "You must stay in the house and save your strength."

He takes her hand and lays it over his chest, and she smiles her slow smile. The sight of her face brings him joy, as it always has. Yet in her eyes, even as she stares into his own, an unnavigable distance. So it will be, then, unto the end.

He points to the trees, the hills. "Look. As though it were daytime, as though night has not come at all, nor ever will."

She nods sorrowfully, understanding him, and stares out at the land. He studies her profile: her high forehead, her strong nose, her soft mouth, the unloosened hair still so black it glints blue.

She turns back to him. "Come. Let us go into the house. Shall I help you?"

He shakes his head. "I wish to remain here."

She sits quietly for a moment, then lies down next to him. "Are you hungry?"

"No."

From the bodice of her gown she pulls out a small cloth and unfolds it. "I have brought pistachios. And also I have dates."

"No," he says, more gently.

"Have you great pain?"

"Greatest is the pain that comes from the unanswered question in my heart."

"Joseph. When will you believe?"

"I pray to now."

"Then I shall pray with you, that you may know that what the angels have told you is true."

CHAPTER ONE

. . .

Nazareth

JANUARY, 4 B.C.

Joseph

Outside, a thunderstorm raged. A great wind frightened the animals and bent the trees low to the ground, shaking their leaves almost off their branches. But inside the house of just-married Simon and Esther, there was light and laughter. A long table covered with a striped cloth was pushed up close to the wall, and it was laden with earthenware platters decorated by palm fronds and piled high with eggplant and olives, with spit-roasted beef and lamb and fish, with rounds of flatbread, with grapes and oranges and figs and sweet cakes.

Beneath the table, sixteen-year-old Joseph sat cross-legged in silence, watching sandals and ankles and hems of tunics go by. No one had seen him—he was almost totally obscured by the tablecloth—and he enjoyed the anonymity. He was of course a man now, but he could not resist on occasion returning to the pleasures of boyhood. This was one such pleasure: to sit hidden and watch the elders as they drank ever more wine and acted ever more foolish. In the corner, he saw old Samuel weaving as he stood with his feet far apart, trying to focus on the face before him. Wine had sloshed from his wooden cup to dribble down his mantle. "You will soon be on the floor," Joseph muttered, and was startled to hear a voice say, "I am surprised he is not already."

Joseph turned to see a girl squatting just behind him. "You have found the seat of honor," she said. "May I join you here?"

There was something familiar about her. "We are known to each other?" he asked.

She nodded. "You have seen me many times. And you spoke to me when last you saw me. You came to the well when I was there last summer. I was gathering water with my mother; you were passing by with your father, Jacob."

"Your memory serves you well. And I remember now, also. You are called Mary." She was a wonder to behold, with her black curls escaped from her braid, her cheeks flushed dusky rose, her gaze so direct and yet mysterious. She tucked her hair behind her ears, and he saw the lines of her high cheekbones beginning to assert themselves. Her lips were full and pink. He was suddenly dry-mouthed, his heart knocking about in his chest like a caged animal wild to be released.

"Yes, I am Mary," she said. "And you are called Joseph."

And her voice! Low and musical, laugh-like. The utter completeness of her beauty was astonishing; it made for a rush of emotion in him so strong it felt like anger.

"You have . . . grown," he told her, and his voice cracked, causing him to blush to the center of his soul.

She appeared not to notice but instead stared calmly into his eyes. "And you also."

"How old are you?" he asked.

"Newly thirteen. And you?"

"Seventeen in two days."

They regarded each other carefully, and then he ducked down and pointed to the people before him who had joined hands and made a circle to dance. They whooped and called out to one another, stamped their feet, threw their heads back and laughed. "They rejoice so!" Joseph said, caught between wanting to admire them and to ridicule them. "It is as though King Herod has died and the Messiah has come, both together!"

She came closer and peered from beneath the cloth to see the dancers, then sat next to Joseph. "It makes me happy, their happiness," she said, and there was in her simple statement a truth that made him ashamed of his ambivalence.

"Of course it makes me glad as well," he said. What was it that she smelled of? It was a scent of air and water, of salt and bread, of the white blossoms that flowered on the olive branches. Of apricots and nuts. Of earth. He felt himself growing dizzy. He leaned back onto his elbows and looked at her. "Where are you from?"

She cocked her head, puzzled. "Nazareth."

"No," he said.

She raised an eyebrow. "No?"

He shook his head. "No."

"I am from Nazareth! Unless you mean . . . ah. I was born in Sepphoris, but I came to Nazareth when I was just—"

"No," he said yet again.

She stared at him, then lowered her eyes. "I believe you must know of my extraordinary circumstances." She looked up again. "Is that what you mean to say?"

He shrugged. "Perhaps." He didn't know what he was saying. The girl confused and unsettled him.

She smiled, a warm, rich thing, full of its own intention—he had never seen such a smile. But then her face grew serious. "Behold; by a way known only unto you and God, you have come to know of my great secret, of my strange beginnings. I have never spoken of this to anyone, nor have my parents. But I will reveal all to you if you promise never to tell another. Will you promise?"

He smiled uncertainly. She remained somber-faced and did not speak, waiting for him to agree to what she had asked. "I promise," he said.

She nodded and resettled herself, sitting

back on her heels and again anchoring her hair behind her ears. "So be it. We have agreed that this will be known only to you and to my parents, now and forever, unto the end of the earth."

"Yes." His chest inflated with his importance.

She leaned in closer and spoke quietly. "I was found beneath a date palm tree at the edge of the great Plain of Esdraelon. I was wrapped in cloth spun of gold, wearing a crown of jasmine flowers. Beside me were gifts of incense and linens, of spices and jewels, left for the one who would take me unto herself and raise me as her own."

He tried not to laugh.

"Ah," she said. "I see that you cannot believe. You must not feel ashamed. It takes a man of rare qualities to—"

"I believe," he said. "I do! I believe!"

Now she laughed. "Then you have believed a lie. But the circumstances of my birth are yet more miraculous than what I have told you. My mother, Anne, was barren; but late in her life, an angel appeared before her and said—" Mary stopped and turned her head in the direction of a voice calling her name. Her high brow, her strong nose. "I must go," she told him, pulling up her head covering and starting to crawl away from him.

He put his hand on her back. "Wait!" When Mary turned to him, he found himself frustratingly wordless.

Again, they heard her name being called, more insistently this time.

"I must go!"

"Until the next time!" he managed.

She rose too quickly and knocked her head against the underside of the table, then turned back to Joseph, giggling.

He did not smile. He would kill the table, for hurting her.

He lay down on his stomach to watch her walk across the room. Her gait was slow and easy. She moved with her back straight and her head high, and her bearing suggested something beyond the normally erect posture seen in Nazarene women, who were so used to carrying heavy loads upon their heads. Mary took her mother's hand, then turned to look in Joseph's direction and smiled. His breath was tight, his belly aching. He watched as she and her parents headed out into the rain, then sat up and returned his attention to the flush-faced revelers and silently invited them to his own ceremony, now that he knew with certainty to whom he would be betrothed. It was as though it were written in the stars, and always had been. And always would be.

"Mother?" he called. It was late into the night, and Joseph could not sleep. He had lain for at least an hour turning from one side to the other on his pallet, staring up at the ceiling, occasionally reaching out his hand to run it slowly along the mud wall, cool after the storm. He had touched him-self, lightly and with wonder, understanding now the reason for his manhood.

"Mother!" he called again.

It was his father's frame that suddenly filled the low and narrow doorway. Joseph's mother had become an increasingly sound sleeper. Also she had begun to grow a mustache.

"What is it, my son?" Jacob asked. "Are you ill?"

"No."

"Then why do you call so persistently,

when your mother and I need to take our rest?"

He did not answer, and his father moved closer. "Joseph?"

"When will we see those people again?"

"What people?"

"The people who came to the wedding party tonight."

His father lifted his shoulders and made a sound deep in his throat. "We all live in the same small village. We see one another often."

"No, but . . . the people Anne and Joachim, and their daughter, Mary. When will we see them again?"

"Ahhhhhh," his father said. "Have you interest in Mary?"

Joseph said nothing.

His father clapped his hands together and his voice rose high and tight in happiness. "I have waited long for this moment! I shall invite them to Sabbath dinner next week, that you may look again upon your Mary. And then we shall see what will happen."

"I know already," Joseph said.

His father scratched at his side and yawned. "We shall see. And now you must sleep, that you may grow strong and healthy and into a husband fit to father many sons."

Joseph turned onto his side and closed his eyes.

"I am happy for you, my son."

"And I too, Father."

"Good night, Joseph."

He listened to his father's footsteps move away from him in the dark. Had his father felt this, this reeling sensation, big as all of the heavens, for his now snoring wife? Impossible.

Joseph drew in a deep breath and let it out. He closed his eyes tighter. But still he did not sleep. He saw again every move she made, heard again her every word. And waited for morning, which would bring him one day closer to his own wedding day.

CHAPTER TWO

. . .

Mary

Joseph's mother, Rachel, lit the two candles on the table, then passed her hands slowly over the flickering flames and back toward herself, welcoming in the Sabbath. Covering her eyes, she began reciting, "Barukh atah Adonai, Elohaynu, melekh ha-olam . . ." *Blessed are you, Lord, our God, King of the Universe . . .*

Mary sat with her eyes fixed on her lap, trying to pay attention, but it was of no use. She was too excited: her heart thumped so hard she thought it might be audible, her mind was racing, and she kept feeling as though she might cry out. She drew in a breath and unclenched her fists that she might at least appear calm, sitting here at the table across from the young man to whom she was so strongly drawn.

She and her parents had all but run through the village's narrow alleyways to the home of Rachel and Jacob, but still they had arrived late, thanks to a neighbor's ailing donkey that her father had delayed their departure to attend to. Joachim had a gift for curing animals, and someone was forever coming to him—no matter the hour—with chickens, with sheep, with cows. Once, a little neighbor boy had brought over a sparrow with a broken wing. With meticulous care, Joachim had set the wing, using a twig and a thin strip of cloth. He had then told the child to leave the bird with him; he would watch over it that night. The bird had died, as expected, and at dawn Joachim had buried it. Then he had hidden in the bushes until he caught another sparrow, which he placed in a covered basket and presented to the boy. Joachim told him his bird was cured, and now he should set it free. The boy complied reluctantly; he watched with Joachim as the bird flew furiously away. But then the child began to weep and stomp his feet, saying, "I wanted it for myself!"

Joachim gently admonished the boy, asking, "Which is greater, your desire to have the bird captured, or the bird's need for freedom? Belonging to everyone, as it now does, does it not also belong to you?"

Because Joachim had assisted the donkey in giving birth, the sun was soon to set when Mary and her parents arrived at Joseph's. There had been no time to be shown graciously around his home. But no one could fail to notice that the downstairs of the house had not one room but two, and that it was equipped with many oil lamps; Joseph's father had olive orchards. One could not help but see that Rachel wore a mantle dyed red with madder root, and that the linen of her tunic was whole and without the patches so familiar to Mary and her parents. Joseph had immediately risen higher in Mary's esteem, not only for his family's riches but for the kind way in which he welcomed both her and her parents. He had about him an air of easy confidence that Mary knew her parents admired; they had looked at each other in an approving way after he had spoken to them.

The table had been properly set with two loaves of challah covered with plain white cloths, and with earthenware cups. Rachel had politely accepted the wine Joachim had brought, made with grapes from his own vineyards, and then everyone had sat down immediately so that Rachel could light the candles at the proper time. Now she completed the blessing and uncovered her eyes to look at the candles and to smile at her guests. The light in the room was a pinkish orange from the sun hanging low in the sky, and there was in the air the rich scent of cumin and garlic, of lemon and coriander.

Mary stole another look at Joseph's mother—interesting how in candlelight everyone looked beautiful, even Rachel, whose countenance was overly long and wide, more a man's face than a woman's. But Mary had seen already that Rachel's heart was good and generous, her manner lively, her faith deep. And for all her plainness, she had produced a very handsome son. Joseph was too lean, perhaps, but he was wonderfully tall, with reddish-brown hair and copper-colored eyes fringed with dark lashes a woman would envy. His beard was already thick and even.

After the evening service the parents performed the blessing for the children, placing their hands on their offspring's heads and exhorting Mary to be like Sarah, Rebecca, Rachel, and Leah; for Joseph to be like Ephraim and Menasseh. During the kiddush that followed, Mary felt a rush of longing, as she often did during this prayer, to go *home,* though not to the abode of Anne and Joachim. It was to another home, to a place she could not even imagine, much less describe. "Kiy vanu vacharta v'otanu qidashta mikol ha' amiym," she said softly, along with the others. *Indeed, you have chosen us and made us holy among all peoples.*

Mary felt deep inside herself, felt it more and more, that *all* people were holy, that indeed all the earth, with its humans and its animals, with its rocks and rivers and trees, was holy; and that all the things upon the earth were given to one another in an act of such spectacular grace it was impossible to comprehend. Yet an attempt at such understanding should be what life was devoted to, should be what life was *for,* she believed: let there be a joyful fullness in taking, and also fullness in giving.

She did not speak of these things. She held them unto herself and pondered them. Yet now, looking across the table into the shining eyes of Joseph, she considered that there might be for her one true companion, someone who held in his heart what she guarded so carefully in her own.

When it was Joseph's turn to wash his hands, he filled a cup with water and poured it over the top and bottom of his left hand first. He realized his error immediately and corrected it, pouring again quickly over his right hand and pointedly avoiding looking at Mary. *I am also nervous,* she wanted to tell him. *Do not despair.* And it was as though he heard her thoughts, for he looked up with relief and smiled at her. She smiled back, and again she saw her parents exchange glances.

At last, Jacob moved to the head of the table for the ha-motzi. He pulled the cloth from the two challah loaves and lifted them high into the air while he recited the final blessing in his deep, slow voice: "Barukh atah Adonai, Elohaynu, melekh ha-olam, ha-motzi lechem min ha-aretz." *Blessed are you, Lord, our God, King of the Universe, who brings forth bread from the earth.*

Amein! Mary said silently with him, then watched eagerly as he ripped off pieces of bread for each person and passed them down the table. Mary was suddenly starving, eager for everything before her.

That night, as Mary lay awake on her pallet, her mother came to sit cross-legged beside her. Anne smelled of the rosemary she used to scent the olive oil she rubbed into her heels each evening before bed. The lamp cast shadows on her face, deepening her wrinkles, but still she was beautiful. She stroked her daughter's cheek, pushed a tangle of curls back from her forehead. "Are we at last to make a match, then?"

"At *last,*" Mary muttered. "I am only now turned thirteen!"

"Already thirteen, and never so much as gazed upon a man until now."

Mary said nothing. From across the room came the deep and even sounds of her father breathing. At last, Mary smiled, and with this her mother smiled also, and then the two of them began quietly giggling. "Did you see her mantle?" Mary asked. "The red?"

Her mother shook her head in admiration. "It is said that she has blue, as well."

"No one in all our village has the means for indigo dye!"

Her mother raised an eyebrow.

"No one," Mary said firmly.

"Her vegetable stew was delicious," Anne said. Coming from Mary's mother, this was a rare compliment; usually Anne let people know that although a dish might taste good, it could not compare to her own version. "And she set a fine table."

"Yes."

Her mother reached behind herself to rub a place on her lower back. Then she said, "When you went out with him to the courtyard, of what did you speak?"

Mary blushed. "He told me he had a dream that we were married and had seven children."

"Seven!" Mary's mother cried, and her father turned in his sleep, muttering to himself. "Seven!" she said again, this time in a whisper. "And I suppose all of them were sons!"

"That I do not know," Mary said. "But when I, too, expressed surprise over the number of children he so easily assigned me, he said, 'I see, though, that you voiced no objection to the marriage.' "

"He is clever as well as handsome."

Mary smiled, but then she grew serious. She sat up and took her mother's hands into her own. "Tell me, please. How do you know?"

"Know what?"

"Know when it is time."

"You know it is time when your parents make a match."

Mary's face fell, and Anne leaned in closer. "And you know when your heart beats fast, your breathing quickens, and your dreams are full of your betrothed."

"He is not yet my betrothed!" Mary said quickly.

"Love grows slowly, but steadily," Anne said. "You will come to see this, my daughter. For I believe we shall make a match." She yawned. "And now I shall bid you good rest, and hope for the same myself. Tonight my bones ache."

She kissed Mary's forehead, and Mary lay down, then reached out again for her mother's hand. "Mother?"

"Yes?"

She looked upon Anne's face, beloved to her, deeply familiar. She was full of questions, full of doubt. But she drew in a breath and said only, "I wish you sound sleep."

"You are frightened," Anne said.

Mary nodded.

"Tell me why."

Mary hesitated, then said, "It is . . . new. I am only excited, I think."

"Perhaps you worry that he and his family are too far above us," Anne said. "Ah, Mary. Are you such a poor offering? My only daughter, my beauty. I shall tell you something now. When you were conceived, an angel came to me and said—"

"I *know*," Mary said. "I can tell the story to you!"

"Backward, no doubt," Anne said. "As fine as your beauty is your mind. But what I want to tell you this night is something I have never told you before."

Mary waited.

"I hesitated to reveal these things to you," Anne said, "fearing it would make you swell with pride and be unto others as is dreadful Naomi."

Mary smiled, thinking of her boastful friend who lived nearby and referred constantly to her skill at bread baking and weaving, to the sheen of her hair and her fine form. She reminded Mary of the crowing rooster that strutted back and forth across the courtyard, oblivious of the fact that he was his only admirer. Still, Mary loved her.

"Hear me now," Anne said. "The angel said not only that I would conceive when I was barren, but that my offspring would be spoken of in the whole inhabited world."

Mary breathed out in a rush. "Truly, Mother?"

"For what reason would I lie to one I so love?"

"But . . . how?"

Anne shrugged. "We wait always on God's will. But also we must believe his messengers."

Mary wanted to say something, but what? What would be right to say? *Yes, it is true that I have felt inside myself some call to greatness.* Would that not be even more boastful than Naomi? *Yes, and this is why I feel destined to a fate other than marriage and the life you have lived with Father.* Such words would deeply sadden her mother, and make her think that Mary dishonored her parents, which she did not. And Anne longed so for her daughter to marry— she had spoken of Mary's wedding day since Mary was a little girl. Finally, Mary said simply, "I shall embrace my destiny."

"Such grandchildren I will have!" Anne said. "I pray that I may live to see them have children of their own. All seven of them!" She laughed, but there was a sadness in it. Anne was elderly, and grew every day older. She rose with difficulty from her sitting position onto her knees. "We shall speak of this again in the morning. For now, know that I hold in my heart the wish for your great happiness, as I always have." Again she kissed her daughter, and then she made her way quietly across the room and extinguished the lamp. Mary heard her mother adjusting herself on her pallet, and then all was quiet.

Mary closed her eyes and lay still, thinking of how, outside, the stars glowed in the sky, silent yet revelatory. She wished she could read them, as could the wise men from the east she had heard about. What was her destiny? She knew her mother thought it had to do with Joseph, that she had witnessed tonight the beginning of the fulfillment of the angel's promise. But Mary did not share this belief. Something in her pushed against the notion.

Still. She closed her eyes and saw again Joseph's handsome face. Felt again the thrill she'd experienced when they'd brushed hands, eating from the common bowl. In becoming his helpmate, in helping him to achieve all he was capable of, could she not find her own glory, and be as well in her proper place? She closed her eyes and forced her thoughts to sleep.

CHAPTER THREE

. . .

MARCH

Joseph

Joseph found Mary and her mother sitting out in their courtyard with other neighborhood women, doing laundry. Hidden beneath his girdle was the gift he had finished making for Mary that morning, a small wooden box with an intricate design on the lid. She knew already of his skill as a stonemason; now she would see his talent as a carpenter and woodcarver. "Come for a walk with me," he told her, after he had wished both her and her mother peace.

Mary looked at her mother for permission, and Anne said, "It is for Joseph to decide for you, now."

"According to your will," Joseph told Anne. It would not hurt to move further into her favor.

"You may go," Mary's mother told her. "But when you return, you must pound the wheat, gather herbs, and milk the goats." She returned to scrubbing the laundry, and even with her head bent low, Joseph could see her smile.

Mary rose and dried her hands against her tunic. Then she began to walk with Joseph, gently steering him in a direction that would have them go past Naomi, who sat with her disagreeable mother near the olive press. "Shalom, Joseph," Naomi said as they passed by, and in her words he heard the rest of her thought: *Why her and not me?* He greeted Naomi, then turned to wave at Anne. She waved back, then watched them go, her hand shading her eyes against the already hot morning sun.

It pleased Joseph to know how much Anne liked him, Anne and her husband, Joachim, too. And Mary, who now walked proudly beside him—there was no doubt she liked him! He had seen it even at the wedding party where they first met, but each time he had seen her since, his confidence had grown. He knew that she now cared for him deeply. Two months ago, in a ceremony before family and friends, they had been betrothed according to their parents' will. Joseph had written the ketubah, assigning Mary money in the event of his death. They were now legally man and wife.

On their wedding day, one year after the betrothal, they would enjoy a feast the likes of which had never been seen in their village, said his mother. Already Rachel made herself dizzy every day, talking of how everyone would praise Joseph and Mary's wedding. For years to come they would speak of it! About the handsome groom, the beautiful bride, and she herself (not to take away from the bride, of course) dressed in finery procured in Jerusalem. About the festal fire of brush and tamarisk branches that would light up the sky. About the beauty of the tables laden with food so artistically arranged it would be a shame to eat it. About the fine musicians who would entertain the guests. She spoke of the procession of young women who would escort Joseph by torchlight to the wedding feast, how they would all be weeping and beating their breasts that such a prize was no longer available.

Joseph walked smiling, his heart light. Now he was fully a man. Now his life was rich with purpose and had truly begun. Every morning when he rose from his pallet, a thought came to him like the sun: *Mary.* This winter, she would move in with him and they would live together. And then he would know her. He felt a stirring in his loins and directed his thoughts quickly to the design of their stone house.

Already he had very nearly finished it. And already his skill as a carpenter was becoming well known. He had been asked to join the workers who were putting up new buildings for Herod in Sepphoris. The city was being totally rebuilt, even as was the great temple in Jerusalem—for nearly twenty years men had labored on it, and it was said that it would be well over twenty years more until its completion! He would profit well from his work there. Joseph hoped it brought Mary's parents great joy to know that he would be able to care for their daughter; that she would not want for anything. What went unspoken was that they could now die in peace.

He sneaked looks at Mary as they walked slowly along. It was unusually warm for this time of year, and he didn't want to tax her. She was his prize, his pearl. Mary's great beauty mixed with his own pleasing looks meant that his sons would be handsome. It mattered to him that his sons be handsome and strong, though naturally the strength would come from him.

After a time they came to a creek, and they stopped to rest on its bank. Joseph wiped sweat from his brow and smiled at Mary, who was flush-faced and beautiful in the heat. "I never knew of this place," she said.

"It is a tributary from the Jordan that runs rarely," Joseph said. "Only when we have had a wet winter such as the one that just passed. It will last but a few weeks more. Today it runs harder and faster than I have ever seen."

"And it is loud!" Mary said. "I can scarcely hear the birds." Overhead, they twittered in the trees. Mary watched as they flew from bough to bough.

"You like birds, and indeed all animals," Joseph observed.

"Yes. As does my father." She told Joseph the story of the little boy and the sparrow, and the words her father had spoken.

"I wish you had known me then," Joseph said, "that I might have built a cage for the bird. A pity to disappoint the child."

Mary looked at him, surprised. She started to speak, then said nothing. Instead, she stared into her lap, looking troubled.

What had just happened? Joseph wondered. Whatever it was, it was easily remedied. From his father, he had learned of the power of gifts to a woman. Jacob quieted with great skill Rachel's occasional emotional storms by offering her bits and baubles. It was a weakness in women, the way they were moved by their feelings. A wise man knew how to control this in his mate.

"I have made something for you," Joseph said.

There, the corners of her lips moving up. "Have you?"

He pulled the box from beneath his girdle and presented it to her.

She gasped and traced with her fingers the ornate design on the top. "It is magnificent, Joseph! How are you able to carve these small leaves, these beautiful flowers?"

He leaned back on his elbows and did not answer. She did not want an answer anyway—she merely wanted to express her gratitude. He was deeply satisfied; it was the reaction he had longed for and indeed imagined, down to her touching the images with great wonder and appreciation. In his next carving for her, he would put in a bird.

"How *did* you do it?" she asked.

She really wanted to know! He sat up, amused. "Well, there are tools for such things. And one develops a skill for carving, after a time."

"What tools?" Mary asked. "And how is it that you develop such skills? With what did you begin? Did you first make something for your mother?"

Joseph moved closer to her. "You are full of questions, my wife. Will it ever be so?

Will a man never have rest from working when he is with you?"

She blushed. "Forgive me. I am inspired by your talent. I thank you for my gift, my husband." She smiled then, and he took her hand, and together they enjoyed the breeze that passed over the water and cooled them.

After a few minutes, Mary removed her sandals. She slid closer to the edge of the creek and dipped her feet into the water. Joseph put his feet in, too, but pulled them out immediately, howling from the jolting cold. Mary laughed at him, wiggling her toes with pleasure. Joseph eased his feet back into the water, fighting the impulse to cry out again.

"Shall we go in farther?" Mary asked.

"Into the water?"

She nodded, her eyes mischievous.

"We must not," he said. The creek was narrow, but one could not judge its depth. There was a small current. He could not swim. "We shall get wet, and we must return to the village soon," he told her.

"Of course you are right," Mary said. She moved her feet about, then suddenly reached down and splashed water at

Joseph. He grabbed her hand to subdue her, then pulled it gently onto his breast, over his heart. A great calm came over him. They sat looking at each other, feeling the richness of each other's affection. Then Mary took her hand away to pick a wild-flower and presented it to Joseph. He kissed her fingers and tucked the blossom behind his ear. Mary bowed her head and smiled.

He picked up a stick and, in the dirt be-tween them, wrote something. "What do you think that says?" he asked.

"You know I cannot read." But she peered closely at the marks he had made.

"It says 'Simon.' "

"And the meaning?" she asked.

"The name of our firstborn."

"And if it is a girl?"

"It won't be."

"You are full of confidence!"

He leaned back on his elbows and re-garded her. Then he asked, "Would you like to go on a journey with me? To Sepphoris?"

She clapped her hands together. "Oh, Joseph! Will you take me there?"

"I will."

"When?"

"Tomorrow."

"Always I have wanted to see my place of birth! But never have my parents taken me there."

"It would be hard for them. But not for me."

She pressed her fingers to her mouth and smiled behind them, then leaned over to quickly kiss his cheek. Then she kissed him again, more slowly, and began moving her mouth toward his. He felt her hand come onto his knee.

"Mary," he said. "It is forbidden."

"Joseph," she said. "I care not."

He laughed and pulled away from her, then stood and stretched his arms up high, so her eyes would be focused upward and not on another part of him that also had risen. He was astonished and a little embarrassed by her forwardness. But happy, too, at the hint of pleasures to come. Often enough during the night he had heard his mother's soft protestations—*Jacob! I am so weary!*—followed properly by her cooperation. It was clear that Joseph would not have this problem.

He made his voice go stern and low, manlike. "We must go. Tomorrow we shall complete our chores early in the morning. It is a long walk to Sepphoris and back. And in between, much to see and do."

Mary put her sandals on, then stood and looked up at him. Her head cover was crooked, and Joseph gently straightened it.

All the way back to the village, Mary asked questions about what they would see in Sepphoris, what they would do there. And Joseph told her to be patient, that all her questions would be answered in time.

CHAPTER FOUR

Joseph

Five hundred feet above their village, they could see thirty miles in three directions. Mary stood speechless, the wind pulling at her tunic, looking at the snow-topped mountains to the north, the Sea of Galilee to the east, and the Mediterranean to the west. To the south was the Plain of Esdraelon and the uplands of Gilead and Samaria. On the next hill to the northwest, they could see Sepphoris, the city they were going to walk to. Joseph showed her a road that went all the way to Egypt, as well as Via Maris, the Way of the Sea, a Roman road connecting Damascus with the seaports. Just as they turned to leave, he put his hand on Mary's shoulder and pointed to the minute forms of a caravan that had just come into view. "Look," he said. "They are on their way from Jordan to the city of Caesarea."

"The Silk Road!" she said. "It is the Silk Road I am seeing!"

"An extension of it," he said, smiling.

She turned her attention again to the long, slowly moving line. "What do they carry?"

Joseph shrugged. "Pepper. Saffron. Silk, of course." He was not so much interested in their wares as he was in their route.

"Joseph," she said quietly. "Look what you have given me!" She turned slowly around and around, her face radiant with wonder. He was full of pride, as though he had indeed made all this for her, as though it had not been there for many years before them and would be after.

"I shall show you even more now," he said. "Let us be on our way."

She moved ahead of him through the firs and the cedar trees and down the steep path, thick with thistles. She cried out suddenly, and sat down. A deep gash above her ankle was bleeding freely. She pressed her fingers over the cut, looked quickly about, and then directed Joseph to pick various things for her, wild mint from here, various other leaves from there. She pressed them together and lay them over her wound. Almost immediately the bleeding stopped. Soon afterward, Mary lifted the leaves. No redness to the wound, no swelling. She stood up. "Let us go."

"Does it not hurt you?" Joseph asked.

"Not any longer." She lifted the bottom of her tunic to show him where she had been injured. One could scarcely see a mark.

"It is a miracle. My wife is a miracle worker!"

She laughed. "My husband fails to understand. It is only nature, caring for us as we care for it."

Joseph frowned. "We care for nature? How is that?"

Mary's face grew thoughtful. "We appreciate it. We are mindful of it. For all things on the earth are one. All things are one another's children and also one another's parents. So I believe."

Joseph shook his head and began walking again, this time in front of Mary, that he might prevent another injury to her. Over his shoulder he said, "Never will come the day when we shall have to attend to nature. It cares for itself. Naturally!" He laughed at his own joke and turned around to see Mary enjoying it, too. But she was unsmiling, oddly quiet, looking only at the path before her.

Such a deep-thinking girl, his wife! It was never a good idea to wander so in one's mind. It could make for a restlessness, for deep unhappiness. It would be good when she was busy with their children, attending to those things for which she was created. It was holy, a family, as Mary certainly knew. He and their children would fill her heart and mind so that she would no longer be given to such strange ruminations. Or to asking so many questions!

The walk was five miles over rugged terrain, and the sun beat down upon them. He stopped often to offer Mary water from his goatskin. When she lifted her chin and drank, he admired the loveliness of her long neck, the grace with which she blotted droplets of water from the corners of her mouth, the slow smile of gratitude she offered. Once, walking along beside him,

Mary began to sing. Joseph stopped walking and turned to her.

"What is it?" she asked, looking anxiously about. "What have you seen? A mountain lion?" But there was in her fear a kind of happy excitement.

"No, it is your voice. How lovely it is! I want to be still and listen. Sing for me."

"Ah, but now I shall be too much aware." She looked away from him.

He put his fingers to her chin and gently turned her face toward him. "I ask this of you, my wife."

She looked down and sang the song to completion. Her voice was low and soft; it both soothed and stirred him. She raised her head to look at him, pink-cheeked. "So you have it, my husband. A song for Joseph."

He nodded. "I shall ask that from this day forth, you sing only for me. And for our children."

Her mouth opened, surprised. But then she nodded obediently, and they continued on their way.

● ● ●

When they reached the outskirts of Sepphoris over two hours later, Mary exclaimed, "But this is not far! I could go farther. Then farther yet!"

"And so you will," Joseph said. "We are not yet to the marketplace, nor to any of the buildings I want to show you." He himself was tired from the climb up the hill outside Nazareth and then the long walk. Of course God knew it took a toll to walk a distance watching out for someone else! As her protector, he had walked the distance twice. He would be glad to sit for a while and eat some of the delectable food offered at the marketplace. He wanted especially some of the skewered meat that had been marinated in herbs and oils, then grilled.

Mary turned to face him. "I could walk to the Sea of Galilee!"

He laughed. "It seems I have perhaps shown you too much. For now you are full of foolishness!"

"But could I not?"

He tipped his head left and right in a gesture of equivocation. "You *could,* perhaps. But would it be wise? No. It would be unwise, indeed."

"Have you seen it?"

"The Sea of Galilee? Yes. I went there once, with my father."

Her eyes widened. "What is it like?"

"It is like . . . a sea."

"Joseph!"

"All right, my demanding one. It is . . . it is bluer than one could ever imagine. A blue that both incites the imagination and calms the spirit. And vast beyond comprehension. Sunlight sparkles on the water bright as all of Caesar's jewels; it stabs the eyes; and fishermen shout and—" He hung his head, shook it, and slowly began to laugh.

"What?" Mary asked. "What do the fishermen do?"

"Mary. Why do you stand with your back to your birthplace, which we have traveled so far to see? We are in Sepphoris! Let us appreciate what is before us!"

"You are right as always, my husband." Mary turned around, reached back for Joseph's hand, and together they walked into the city.

Because of Mary's delight, Joseph saw with new eyes the colorful chaos of the multicultural marketplace: fortune-tellers; gangs of running children, their faces smeared with food; coins being flung onto silver platters; sheep being herded through the crowd, the whites of their eyes showing in panic; toothless beggars; turtledoves cooing from wooden cages; stall after stall of vendors loudly hawking bolts of linen, scented olive oil, watermelon, metal oil lamps, mantles, tunics, and cloaks.

As they walked the streets, they admired the Roman architecture of the banks and law courts, the Greek mosaics with their representations of people and animals, of flowers and leaves and winding vines. At last, Joseph stopped before one half-finished building and pointed. "There it is!" he said proudly.

She stared. "There *what* is?"

"The building I am working on! The one I told you about. It was I who cut and laid those stones in the corner!"

"Ah!" she said.

"And also I shall make the door for it." He felt foolish now.

Mary hesitated, then said, "You alone will do that?"

He shrugged.

She moved closer to the building. "It will be a *fine* door!" she said loudly, and her loving enthusiasm raised his spirits.

"Now we shall go back to the market-place and eat," he said. She ran to his side and looked up at him. "Shall we have honey cakes?"

As they ate, they sat on a half-wall and watched the activity in the marketplace. Most of the people were unlike the lean specimens in Nazareth—they had plump bellies and soft-looking hands, faces absent of the deep wrinkles so common to Nazarenes. Their garments were made from fine wools and silks, and Mary stared longingly at the bright colors. People spoke loudly in many foreign languages. Even the Aramaic spoken here was different—so many dialects, and all far less guttural than the language Mary and Joseph used.

Mary pointed to a handsome man a short distance away, who stood talking to a circle of admiring onlookers.

"Who is that?" she asked, talking around the honey cake in her mouth.

Joseph tenderly brushed a crumb from her face. "It is a traveling teacher, one who makes his way from town to town accept-

ing gifts from those who come to see him."
There was in his explanation a measure of
contempt.

"But . . . he is a disciple, then, is he not?"

"No," Joseph said.

"A scribe?"

"He is not a Jew."

Mary looked at him. "But he is a teacher."

"So they call themselves. But they believe not as we do. Our Torah and Mishna
stress religion, law, history, and ethics. The
Greek gymnasium concerns itself with
science, the arts, linguistics, and body
training."

"But is that wrong?" Mary asked. "The
Roman government allows everyone to
practice what they believe."

"Yes," Joseph said. "But the Romans
view all these beliefs as being part of their
own system! And they meddle in our affairs
when it is our right and our desire to be
separate." He watched the teacher gestur-
ing wildly to make a point. "That man's
teachings are dangerous."

"Why?"

Joseph sighed. It was unseemly, the girl's
inquisitiveness. But he would share with her
what he had learned at synagogue, that she

might be impressed by how he, too, could speak in a teacher's way. "It is dangerous because it harkens back to the time of the Cynics," he told her. "Hundreds of years ago, they called for a lifestyle of austerity and self-sufficiency. They encouraged both men and women to renounce all claims of the state and the social order. Even the family and religion were to be rejected in favor of a free life in accordance with 'nature'! Such teachings were of course a threat to order and morality, and the Cynics were expelled from Rome long ago. Now there are those who are beginning to speak again of such things."

"Let us listen." Before Joseph could stop her, Mary rose and moved closer. The traveling teacher saw her and stopped talking and stared; even in a place so cosmopolitan as this, Mary's beauty shone. He smiled at her, and she looked down and tucked her escaped hair behind her ears. She would need to perfect her braiding, Joseph thought. Only on her wedding day should a woman's hair be loose.

He came to stand at Mary's side. "We must go now. The hour grows late, and we must be back in Nazareth before dark or tempt the wild animals."

They walked rapidly at first; then, as the city grew smaller in the distance, more slowly. Mary asked Joseph about the construction of the buildings. About the lives of the buyers and the sellers they'd seen in the marketplace. About whether he had ever dreamed of being a scribe—what an honor it would be, did he not agree? Only once did Joseph lose patience with her, and that was when she asked if they might live in Sepphoris.

"No," he said.

"You would be close to the place where you labor. You would not have to walk so far each day . . ."

"We will never live in Sepphoris." He would not look at her.

". . . and you would be quicker coming home to me." Her voice was singsong, flirtatious.

"It is forbidden!"

"Forbidden? By whom? I think only by you."

Joseph stopped walking and turned to her. "What did you say?"

Mary did not repeat herself. But there was no need; Joseph had heard her.

"Always we will honor our traditions," he said. "And we will raise our children in the village where we ourselves were raised." He began walking again.

Mary spoke softly, wearily. "Never have I said we would not honor our traditions."

For some time, they walked without speaking. And then Mary reached again for Joseph's hand. Somewhere inside, she acknowledged her own wrongheadedness. Joseph was only doing what he should, pushing her to become a proper woman, a proper wife. She should stop asking questions, talking back, taunting him. He was tall and handsome, kinder than any man she had ever known. His kisses rattled her to the bone. Even in anger he never frightened her; she saw him those times as a puppy holding on to his end of the rope. When they were wed, surely she would want for nothing.

CHAPTER FIVE

. . .

Mary

"Aiy!" Mary reached for the back of her head, where Naomi had pitilessly yanked on her hair. Mary sat on the ground, while Naomi kneeled behind her, attempting to fashion a braid that would subdue Mary's curls.

"Do not complain," Naomi scolded. "If Joseph wants your hair done properly, you must learn to do it!" Her voice lowered as she added, "And he is right. Since I have known you, your hair has been wild about your face."

"I know well how to braid my hair," Mary said. "But my hair knows well how to escape. Shall I spend all my days trying to capture it?"

"How often must you be told that wives should at all times endeavor to please their husbands? As women, it is our calling and our privilege. You do not deserve to be betrothed to Joseph! Another woman would know her great fortune!" She yanked again on Mary's hair.

Yola, Mary's other, more favored friend, rose from where she had been lying in the long grass next to the creek. She walked over to the two girls, then seized Mary's braid away from Naomi.

"*Aiy!*" Mary cried again.

Yola loosened her grip and began instead to play gently with Mary's hair, as when they were little girls, and Mary closed her eyes in relief and pleasure. "There is no need for such constraint," Yola said. "Is it not a pleasing sight, Mary's hair about her face? Let us put flowers in her braid instead." She knelt behind Mary, plucked a beautiful white wildflower, and tucked it into her braid. Then she put in another.

Naomi picked a tiny pink flower. "Use this, instead. Pink is better suited to her coloring. White suits *me*."

Yola ignored Naomi's outstretched hand and instead picked another white blossom. "This color is more pleasing." She held it to her nose and breathed in deeply. "And it smells of heaven, besides."

Naomi crossed her arms and stuck out her lips, pouting. "Mary, do you say white or pink?"

Mary shrugged. "Of what significance is the color of flowers I cannot see?"

"They are for *Joseph*!" Naomi and Yola said together. They looked at each other and smiled. On this point, at least, they agreed.

Mary pulled away from Yola and turned to sit opposite her. "Why do we waste our time this way? Let us go into the water and cool ourselves."

The two girls looked at the creek, then at Mary.

"It is too cold," said Naomi.

"It could be deep," said Yola.

"My friends have left me," Mary said. "And have been replaced with old women afraid of their shadows." She moved to the edge of the creek, took off her head cover, and flung it aside. Then she waded into the water, shrieking with delight as the cold rushed over her ankles. She walked in farther.

"You are *wet* now!" Naomi cried, and Yola and Mary laughed at her.

"She should be dry, sitting in a creek?" Yola asked. For Mary had indeed sat down, and now the water reached her chest. This is what she had longed to do when she was here with Joseph.

"Come out from there immediately!" Naomi said. She spoke loudly, that Mary might hear her over the rushing sounds of the water. "It is improper, what you do! Come out before we are seen!"

Mary ignored her.

"We must *go*!" Naomi said.

Mary turned away. On the opposite bank grew more flowers, yellow ones.

Now Yola called out, "Mary! We have stayed too long!"

Exasperated, Mary turned to face her friends. She called back, "Why can you not enjoy this rare pleasure? When I brought you here, I thought surely you would indulge yourselves!"

"Enough!" Naomi said. "I shall have no part of this. I am going back to the village."

She turned and walked quickly away, toward home.

Yola stood hesitating, then moved to the edge of the creek, where she crouched down to speak to her friend. "Naomi has for once spoken truly. It is not fitting, what you do. Come, let us all walk back to the village together."

"I care not what Naomi says. Nor you." Mary swirled her hands about in the water.

Yola frowned. "You are no longer yourself. It is not your friends who are leaving you; it is you who are leaving us."

Mary rose up and sloshed through the water toward Yola, then heaved herself onto the bank. She shook her hands, drying them, and Yola leapt up and away from the flying droplets. "You are wet as the creek itself," she said, laughing. "And your tunic blackened with mud! Your mother will be displeased."

With this Mary did not argue. Her mother would be displeased. She looked down at herself and sighed deeply.

Yola spoke quietly. "What lies in your heart, Mary? Since becoming betrothed, you are changed. You seem to me not joyful but disappointed. Yet Joseph is a good man, handsome, honorable, and hardworking. Devoted to God. And a descendant of the house of David!"

Mary scoffed, "There are many such descendants. There were many harems!"

"Yet we know that the Messiah will come from such a descendant. One of your seven children might be the one we have so long awaited!"

Mary picked a blade of grass and began to peel long strips from it.

"Many are the girls in the village who envy you," Yola said. "Why, Naomi said that Joseph's eyes—"

"I care nothing about what Naomi says." All her friends, even Yola, spoke to her only of Joseph. Mary preferred the way Yola used to be, when they did things other girls wouldn't do: climbing the limestone rocks that surrounded their village, begging apricots from the merchants at the marketplace, laughing at Naomi's mother when her back was turned, spying on the newly betrothed who believed themselves alone in the olive orchards. Even trying to eavesdrop, when the men met to argue the Torah.

"Come, Mary. I grow weary waiting for you."

"I shall not!" Mary looked quickly over at her friend, then apologized.

"I must go without you, then." Yola took a few steps, then turned to look over her shoulder. "Are you coming?"

Mary stared into her wet lap and peeled more strips from the blade of grass. She would peel until it disappeared before her.

"Mary?" Yola called.

"I wish to be alone for a while!" she called back. "And in any case I must wait until my clothes dry before I return to the village. Go without me."

Yola began running to catch up with Naomi. Mary watched her until she disappeared, then began undoing her braid. Her hair, too, was soaked. She would let it dry, rebraid it—properly!—and walk back to the village. And then no more would she unloosen her hair and wade in water. Her days of freedom were over. She must now turn her attention to the duties that lay before her, those that came with being promised to a man. She stood, hesitating, then stepped into the water one last time. She moved to the center of the creek and again sat down. The coolness was exhilarating.

Her tunic floated around her like an immense flower, and she was its center.

A man's voice startled her. And then from behind the bushes appeared the traveling teacher she had last seen in Sepphoris. What was he doing here? Surely no one in Nazareth had offered him gifts for his teaching! He lifted his chin at her, then spoke softly in a language she could not understand—Greek, she thought. She shook her head: *I do not understand you.* She pushed awkwardly at the skirt of her tunic floating about her, trying to make it stay down.

The man laughed, a harsh sound, and then, as Mary watched in horror, he stepped out of his sandals and removed his girdle. She rose quickly, intending to run, then immediately sat back down, for her tunic clung to her most immodestly.

"Please cover your eyes until I have left this place." She doubted the man would oblige her, but she knew of nothing else to do.

He made a face at the sound of her Aramaic. Mary remembered Joseph telling her that Nazarenes were looked down upon almost everywhere for their cruder dialect, for

their simple, uncultured ways, for their preferred isolation and their devotion to tradition. She felt a strong urge to defend her
town, and an equally strong, shameful one,
to say that she had been born in Sepphoris.

The man stood smirking, his hands on his
hips, then stepped into the creek. Slowly,
he began moving toward her. Mary rose,
the water making a sucking sound, and
moved as quickly as she could toward the
opposite bank. How far away were her
friends? If she called for them, could they
hear her? Even as she asked herself this
question, Mary knew the answer. She had
spent too long feeling sorry for herself, re-
gretting the loss of freedom that came with
her betrothal to Joseph, whom she now
wanted in the deep and primal way she
used to want her mother on nights she
burned with fever.

Trying to climb up the slippery rocks,
Mary fell. She slid on her stomach back into
the water, and her tunic rose high above her
waist. She stood quickly, deeply embarrassed, and looked back at the man. He
was not yet upon her, but he had moved
closer. Now he was sitting, his arms
swirling the water lazily about him, his own

tunic risen high about him. He laughed and mockingly showed her his upturned hands.

Mary stood still for a long moment, calculating the distance between them, then scrambled up the bank and ran screaming for Yola and Naomi, for Joseph. She screamed over and over, until it seemed her throat might bleed.

She ran until she could run no more, her wet clothes dragging on her. The man had not followed her—she had looked several times over her shoulder. She stood panting, her heart racing. This is what came of her foolish desire for something beyond what Joseph had offered her. Her sin was her pride, and her sin was now compounded. To have had a man see her so! To have left herself open to being compromised; indeed to have invited such danger! Often she had heard of shepherd girls who had been attacked by Roman soldiers who took advantage of their isolation. She wanted only to go home, yet she knew that when she arrived there, her mother's anger would descend rightfully upon her.

She collapsed into the grass and began to weep. What was wrong with her? Why could she not be happy about her upcoming marriage to a man she deeply cared for and admired, who would be a good father and provider? What did she *want* so? On and on she wept, her hands over her face, her back bowed. She knew not what she wanted, she had alienated her friends, she had experienced an event most fearful, and now she would displease her mother, whom she loved so well.

Then, mercifully, miraculously, it began to rain. Mary felt the drops first on her back, then on her head. *Rain!* Now she could explain her wet clothes and the lateness of her arrival to her mother. She would say that she had stopped to seek shelter but then decided to run home, losing her head cover in the process. And run home she must; surely by now Anne was greatly worried. Mary rose to her knees and in so doing spotted a patch of sage growing nearby. She would eat of it, for she knew it had properties to clear the head. She must only be cautious not to eat too much, for then it was said to cause a rare sort of delusion.

When she arrived in the village, the rain had stopped and the sun was out and beginning its descent; Mary had been gone for many hours. Anne first berated Mary, then embraced her and sent her immediately to lie down—she was still wet and shivering, and Anne feared illness. Mary was grateful for this; it would mean she would not have to speak to her mother when she was feeling so peculiar. She walked on feet that felt not quite her own toward her pallet.

Anne busied herself near the oven, and Mary lay still, comforted by the rich, golden light that had begun to stream into the house through the windows high up on the walls, by the rhythmic sounds of food preparation. Why had she not seen the redemption and beauty in such tasks before now? She would devote herself to keeping a home and caring for children. And she would honor Joseph, who cared for her so well. Never again would she make herself vulnerable to an experience such as the one she had just had. Mary closed her eyes and held back more tears, though these were tears of a different kind.

And then she heard a low voice, saying, "Hail, Mary. The Lord is with you; you are blessed among women." She sat up and clutched the top of her tunic. She wanted to call out to her mother, who had moved to the courtyard, but found she could make no sound. Before her was a towering presence—a man? An *angel*? From behind him came an illumination so intense Mary could not look directly at him. In addition to a terror that caused her to tremble and fight for her breath was a rapturous wonder, a great joy unlike anything she had ever experienced. She felt awakened from a deep sleep, profoundly known. And she felt eerily suspended, yet anchored, in a place she had longed for since birth. She stared out unblinkingly toward the presence, rapt. All the world seemed to have stilled to accommodate this moment.

"Do not be afraid," the angel said. "You have found great favor with God. Now you have conceived in your womb and will bear a son."

But these words! What was he saying? Mary found her voice and spoke most strongly. "How can this be? I have known no man!" Then she gasped and closed her eyes against the vision of herself sitting in the water, her tunic floating about her.

The angel said, "The Holy Spirit will come unto you, and the power of the Most High will overshadow you. Therefore the One born unto you will be the Son of God, and of his kingdom there will be no end."

Mary lay her hand over her throat. Now her voice was barely a whisper. "It is not possible."

"With God, all things are possible," said the angel. "Behold, your cousin Elizabeth was barren, but she has conceived a child and is now in her sixth month. I bid you go to Judea, where you will see for yourself."

"I shall," Mary said, and she meant with her words to communicate her disbelief, her intention to go to Judea to disprove the angel's words. But at that moment her spirit lifted and her heart opened, and there came to her a great sense of relief. And with it came irrefutable knowledge. She understood that what the angel had told her was true, even as the reddening sky outside her window was true. As such, it was not hers to accept or reject. It was a miracle given her by God, told to her by his messenger. She lay her hands in her lap. "I am the handmaid of the Lord," she said. "Let it be with me according to your word."

From behind her, she heard her mother's voice. "Mary? To whom are you speaking?" Anne moved closer, her face full of concern. "Oh, Mary, you must be with fever that your face glows so!" She moved quickly to kneel beside her daughter and put her hand against Mary's forehead. Then Anne grew perplexed, saying, "Yet you are cool to my touch." She lay the back of her fingers against one of Mary's cheeks, then the other.

Mary put her hand over her mother's and looked at her with great tenderness. "Mother," she said. "There is something I must tell you."

"Have you all you need?" Mary's mother asked the next day. Joachim nodded. He was full of sorrow and confusion, as he had been since Anne told him of the angel who had come to their daughter. But he had agreed to accompany Mary to Judea.

"Choose your words well when you speak to Joseph and his family," Joachim told his wife.

Anne smiled. "Of course I shall. Remember that I, too, know of messages from angels."

"Mother," Mary said. She regretted suddenly not having revealed everything that had happened to her yesterday. She had not told Anne about the Greek, though this was not to deceive her mother but to protect her. Now Mary wondered if she had been wrong in this, if she should tell her mother of that experience after all. And surely she should offer some words that her mother might bring to Joseph. But no words would come.

Anne embraced Mary, then kissed her forehead. "Stay with Elizabeth and help her until her child is born."

Mary understood. It would take long for a resolution to be agreed upon. Joseph would not yet be receptive to any words from her. She would wait on the will of God, and hope with all her heart for Joseph's understanding.

"Are you ready, my daughter?" Joachim asked. Their donkey, loaded with supplies, shook his head against a fly, and his harness jingled. There was a sad gaiety in the sound: the excitement of a journey tempered by the reason for it.

Mary nodded, and then she and her father began their long walk south. It would take four days or more to arrive at the home of Zechariah, the ancient priest, and his equally elderly wife, Elizabeth, Mary's cousin, whom the angel had vowed was with child. For a long while Mary and her father did not speak, each busy with thoughts of the journey ahead, and beyond.

CHAPTER SIX

. . .

Judea

Mary

They came out of Samaria and into the hills of Judea in late afternoon and, tired and thirsty, made their way to the house of Elizabeth and Zechariah, who lived just outside of Jerusalem. Joachim watered and tethered the donkey, and Mary pushed open the door of the house, calling her cousin's name.

Elizabeth appeared and, beaming, rushed forward to greet her visitors. "Joachim! Mary! How wonderful to see you!" She stopped suddenly and put her hand to her side, and Mary saw that what the angel had said of Elizabeth was true. "My child moved so within me!" Elizabeth said, laughing. She moved to embrace Joachim and then took Mary's face between her hands, smiled, and touched foreheads with her. Then her face grew full of wonder as she said, "You, too, are with child! Bless you and the fruit of your womb!"

Mary stepped back, saying nothing. Beside her, her father hung his head.

Elizabeth's eyes widened. "And I see, too, that your child will be most exceptional! Oh, Mary! How am I so blessed that the mother of my Lord has come to visit me? Even the child in my womb leapt with knowing when he heard your greeting! Joachim, Joachim, is it not wonderful?"

Joachim lifted his head and nodded at Elizabeth. He did not speak. Tears shone in his eyes.

Mary's heart ached for her father, who, despite their many talks on their journey, did not know what to think or whom to believe. All he knew was that his daughter, his most cherished, was with child, thus endangering both herself and her family. Also, albeit through no fault of her own, she had spoiled her betrothal, about which he had so often and so widely bragged. He feared what would happen when she returned. Women accused of adultery were stoned.

Elizabeth lay her hand over her heart and spoke softly to Mary. "And you are blessed, too, to believe that what the Lord has said will be accomplished."

A deep feeling of love came over Mary then, and with it came a sense of great confidence. She would now be mother to her father, and comfort him. She stood straighter. "Yes, Elizabeth. And my soul magnifies God in praise of him. For he has come to me, a girl who is poor and undistinguished in any way. Despite my circumstances, he has honored me most profoundly, and the child within me is his own. He is all mighty, and for generations many have feared him because he has brought down those who are prideful; even rulers have fallen from their thrones. But in me, he has lifted up the humble. Through me, he will satisfy the hungry. Because of my child, he will have shown Israel mercy, as promised. From now on I shall be not scorned but called blessed, even as you have called me so. I am full of grace."

Now Joachim wept openly, and Mary turned to embrace him. "Do not despair,

Father," she said. "I am strong and happy and clear in my mind. Take your rest and nourishment here, and then leave me with Elizabeth; you see that she understands."

"How goes it with your mother?" Elizabeth asked Mary early the next morning. Joachim had left a short while ago, fortified by a breakfast of hummus and flatbread and grapes, and now she and her cousin sat in the as-yet empty courtyard, the sun bright above them. Mary knew what Elizabeth meant by her question. *What does your mother think about all of this?*

"She, too, was visited by an angel, and in this way told she was with child," Mary said. She was weary to her bones; she had slept poorly, and the exalted confidence she'd felt yesterday was lacking in her this morning. Already she missed her father. She missed Joseph. She missed her mother and her friends.

"Angels come to many, though not all have the courage—or the wisdom—to speak of it," Elizabeth said.

Mary looked over at her. Her face was old

and lined but her eyes clear and wise. She was an intuitionist and an oneiromancer, as well as a great healer. She was known in Judea as the one to come to when one was desperate, when nothing else had worked. Elizabeth had taught Mary's mother much of what she knew about healing, as Anne had then taught Mary. For generations, it had run strong in both sides of Mary's family, such gifts for curing, such strong perceptive abilities.

Elizabeth's compassion was well known, too; those she could not cure she would stay with as they died, easing them back into God's hands. So for all her homesickness, Mary was glad to be with Elizabeth. Mary would help with chores as Elizabeth's time drew nigh, and in return she would be comforted and consoled by her cousin. And educated! Mary knew that now she would pay close attention to the ways of the woman with child, especially when the baby was born. Mary had heard the cries of women in labor, had seen that sometimes the baby died, or the mother, or, saddest of all, both.

She shivered at the idea despite the heat, and Elizabeth, knowing her thoughts,

smiled kindly at her. "There is much to con-
sider, my child. But in this, as in all things,
each day comes one at a time. No matter
our urging, the crops will not grow but according to their own schedule. You will
learn patience. You will come to understand
the thing that has happened to you, and
why. You will learn what to expect when
your own time comes; I will teach you ways
of easing discomfort. When you return
home, it will be not as a child but as a
woman."

Mary nodded, relieved, but then began to
weep. She surprised herself in this. "Forgive me," she said, the urge to laugh vying
with the urge to cry harder.

Elizabeth reached out to put her hand on
Mary's shoulder. "It is the way of women
with child, that their emotions run strong
and with great variation. Much has been
thrust upon you. Yet be not ashamed, and
ask no one's forgiveness." She leaned
closer to Mary. "For I say to you again, you
are blessed."

Mary smiled gratefully.

"Tell me again of the angel," Elizabeth
said, leaning back on her hands and showing Mary a face full of eagerness, as though

she were a child ready to hear her favorite story.

Once more Mary described the event as best she could, and Elizabeth listened carefully and with great pleasure. Her eyes did not widen in awe, she did not scoff and decry Mary's words, she did not protest the likelihood of such an event. She knew of aberrant voices of instruction, of events beyond understanding. And when Mary had finished her story, Elizabeth said simply, "So be it. Now let us eat, for my child demands nourishment." She rose to go back inside, and Mary followed her.

The weeks passed. Oftentimes when he arrived home, Zechariah brought pomegranate juice from the marketplace for Elizabeth. It was her favorite, and he spoiled her now. He offered her back rubs every night, and also he washed her feet, since she could no longer reach past her swollen middle to do it herself. Across from her at the table, he gazed upon her with deep love, seeing not just Elizabeth but their nascent family. He had lost his voice, and so he spoke neither to Mary nor Elizabeth; but no words were needed to communicate his rich devotion.

Mary watched all this with a heavy heart. Would that she were so tenderly cared for by her own husband! For she now felt unwell much of the time. Early every morning she went quietly out into the field behind the house and vomited. The herbs she knew about for treating nausea did not work for her now. She did not speak of her illness to her hosts, for she had been brought there to assist them. Instead, she tiptoed back into the house and returned to her pallet. Later, when Zechariah and Elizabeth ate breakfast, Mary joined them, eating as well as she could the foods Elizabeth insisted were necessary for the growing child inside her: Spinach. Figs. Almonds and eggs.

Elizabeth napped often in the day, and Mary napped, too, sleeping for long hours and dreaming of home. One afternoon, dreaming of sitting beside her mother in the courtyard as they wove with their shuttles, Mary awakened herself weeping. When she opened her eyes, she saw Elizabeth kneeling quietly beside her. She sat up hastily, embarrassed that she had disturbed her cousin's rest, which she now badly needed—her time was close. She tried to compose herself, but the tears would not stop.

"It seems we are in for a summer storm," Elizabeth said, smiling, and her eyes crinkled at the corners. "Have no fear; I mind your tears not at all. It will be a pleasure to attend to you, after you have cared for me so long and so well."

"I know not why I weep," Mary said.

With great care, Elizabeth lowered herself into a sitting position. "Is it such a surprise that a young wife would miss her husband?"

Mary wiped at her eyes, shaking her head. "No."

"Of *course* 'no'!"

"But Elizabeth, I not only miss him, I am full of regret about dishonoring him! I did not cherish him. I resented our betrothal. I told my friends he was too lean, too stern, too bound by tradition. Often I walked in sadness and terrible confusion. I was not grateful for my good fortune, I did not appreciate enough the happy times I had with him, I felt that I was being robbed of my girlhood, of my *youth*!" She began to weep again, loudly. "Oh, Elizabeth, what am I to do? I was undeserving of such love!"

Elizabeth sat quietly for a time. Then she said, "I know well what we must do. First we must call for the slave whips of Herod, that you might more fully punish yourself."

"I speak the truth!" Mary said. "And there is more." She hesitated, then told Elizabeth of what had happened at the creek, how the man had come into the water with her, how only by the miracle given by God was her folly converted to a blessing.

Now Elizabeth's voice grew warm and kind. "Ah, Mary. It was not this unfortunate incident that made you with child! Rather it is the miracle the angel spoke of that brought life to your womb. Few are the people who understand and truly accept miracles; let yourself, at least, be one of them!

"As for Joseph, do you think you are the first to feel this way? Many young women suffer such pangs of doubt! One night, just after I was betrothed to Zechariah, I wept myself unto illness, to think that I would so soon be lost. For that is how I thought of it: in marriage, I would be lost to myself, all my longings and desires subject to the rule of my husband."

"Yes," Mary said.

"Yet we long to be lost in the love of another human being; this also is true, no? For in this way, we are found." Elizabeth reached out and gently touched Mary's cheek. "Such are the ways of life and love. You will come to see how we live so paradoxically. We are happy, yet we are sad. We become enraged by our beloved because he *is* our beloved. We look forward to something, yet we are full of dread. We long for summer in winter, and winter in summer. What a contrary species are we! Better we should be cattle, at peace in the fields!" She grimaced and Mary laughed.

"But mostly in this life," Elizabeth said, "we are continually lifted by the love of God, by the miracles he so freely bestows upon us, and by his nearness to us."

Mary fell silent, thinking, then asked, "But how will Joseph ever believe me, that I am a virgin and yet with child?"

"It is a mountain that has risen in your path, it is true. It would be natural for Joseph to doubt you, even as Zechariah first doubted me. When I told him of the angel appearing to tell me I was with child, he became angry and shouted that I had long been barren. And he reminded me that my years for childbearing were now long past. But then, on the day when he had been chosen to burn incense in the holy place, the angel came to him in the synagogue, telling him that in my womb was a child who would be called John. Yet Zechariah doubted even the angel's words. He questioned him and asked for a sign! Imagine!"

Mary cast her eyes downward, remembering her own questioning of the angel who had appeared to her.

"Yes, my husband, the priest, doubted the truth of the angel's words! And so the angel punished Zechariah. When he came out to speak to the people who had gathered for prayer, he realized he had been struck dumb. There was his sign! The angel said Zechariah will recover his voice when the child is born and named. It is for this reason that my husband does not speak. He was full of worry that I might reveal to you the circumstances of his condition, for he is shamed by the appalling lack of faith he showed. I trust you will not betray my confidence."

Mary shook her head. "Of course I shall not. But how awful! Were you frightened when your husband was struck dumb? Were you terribly sad?"

Elizabeth hesitated. Then her left shoulder met her ear and she raised an eyebrow. "To tell the truth, it isn't so bad."

They laughed, and then Elizabeth put her hand on Mary's arm. "You must explain something to Joseph. Say to him, many are the ways that children come unto us, for mysterious are the ways of the Lord. He may not believe, at first, in the circumstances of your condition. But speak to him of how both of you must want the child who is come, for this is a thing deserved by all who sleep in the womb."

"Yet I cannot help but wonder if he has now lost the love he had for me, if he will still take me as his wife."

Elizabeth shrugged. "Who can guess at what is in another's heart? The things greatest to us are the things we cannot see. I speak here of honor. Truth. Faith. And the greatest of all, which is love. Yet invisible though it may be, when you look upon Joseph again, you will see immediately if love is there."

She grimaced again, then squeezed Mary's arm hard.

"Oh!" Mary said. "Is it time?" Her heart rose in her throat.

Elizabeth nodded. "Help me up."

Mary did, then spoke calmly, saying, "I shall help you to your bed, and then fetch the midwife."

"Make haste," Elizabeth said, around an enormous push.

"Another blessing on us all!" Zechariah shouted. He took a drink of wine from his cup and once more slapped the back of his beleaguered round-bellied friend. From the doorway of the house, Mary watched the small but rowdy group of men standing in the courtyard and celebrating. They had stayed outside as Elizabeth labored, for their place at that time was out of the way of the midwife and her attendants. But once John was born, and Elizabeth and the baby had been bathed and anointed, massaged and celebrated, Zechariah had been allowed in for a look. He'd exchanged some words with Elizabeth, held and admired his son, and then hurried outside to announce to his friends that the baby had come safely into the world. And now was announcing it again and yet again. Mary was beginning to fear for the man who stood beside Zechariah, who'd begun to flinch whenever Zechariah moved. Still, one had to allow dispensation for his behavior: a son was born this night of his wife, Elizabeth. The miracle that had been promised had occurred. And his voice was most robustly returned. "Is not John the very image of myself?" Zechariah bellowed.

"It is so," said one of the men. "If you look a way entirely different from what you have thus far revealed!"

Zechariah stared blearily at him as the other men hooted and laughed. "Your words make no sense, and small wonder. For you are *drunk*!" Then he cried, "I am a thousand times blessed, for unto me this day is born a son!" He lifted his face to the night sky and howled at the moon, and his friends howled with him.

Mary smiled and returned to Elizabeth's bedside. Her cousin lay sleeping soundly, the baby in her arms, and he was sleeping, too. Mary watched them for a long while, then crept silently to her pallet. There, she lay her hands over the small rise of her stomach, and finally slept herself.

In the morning, as Zechariah prepared breakfast, Mary tiptoed to Elizabeth's pallet, where she lay awake and smiling, the baby in her arms. Mary knelt down to see him. He, too, was awake, satisfied-looking after his session at his mother's breast.

"Would you like to hold him?" Elizabeth asked, and Mary nodded shyly, then reached down and took up the baby. He was breathtakingly light. Mary had held babies before, but never one so new as this. Not even a day old! John lay still, and in his eyes was a calm and an acceptance that seemed oddly wise. Mary had never seen such an expression in a baby's eyes before, but then she supposed that one never looked at babies so carefully as did a woman blessed by her own child growing within. Would her baby's toes spread so comically? Would his abdomen rise and fall so rapidly with his breathing, so heartbreakingly? Would his tiny fingers pull at his face, would he fall asleep at her breast with such ease? When she laid him out on her lap to inspect him for the first time, would her face radiate happiness with the intensity that Elizabeth's had? Last night, when Elizabeth, exhausted, had first been given her newborn, his cord still attached, Mary had stood beside her to regard him. John's head was elongated, his nose flattened, and one eye swollen shut. He was covered with blood and vernix. Mary and Elizabeth agreed wholeheartedly on his great beauty. They spoke to the baby in the high, sweet voices given to women for such things.

This morning John's face had already greatly healed, and he truly was beautiful. Looking at him, Mary felt her eyes fill with tears. She handed him carefully back to his mother and then rose, clasping her hands before her. They felt so empty now, her hands, so strangely idle. "I have never seen anything so perfect as this child," she told Elizabeth.

Her cousin looked up at her. "Soon you will see something more perfect still." She spoke sadly then, saying, "I shall miss you, Mary."

"And I you."

"Your traveling companions will soon come for you."

"I am ready."

John suddenly kicked out his legs, wrinkled up his face, and began to cry.

"Kiss me quickly, then, and wait outside, lest we all three cry together," Elizabeth said.

Mary leaned down and kissed her cousin's wrinkled face. "I honor and love you," she said, and Elizabeth answered, "With me as with you. Safe journey, and I bid you give your mother my love and also my thanks, for the assistance of her beautiful daughter."

"It is I who should thank you."

John cried louder, and Elizabeth bent to attend to him.

Mary went to her room for her small bundle of things. She said goodbye to Zechariah, who had packed her a breakfast of flatbread and olives and cheese, and then went outside. The travelers who would journey with her to Nazareth were almost upon her. Mary watched them come.

Soon she would be back in her parents' house. She had grown comfortable here; she loved Elizabeth and Zechariah and now the baby, too. Her health had improved considerably: her cheeks were again flushed pink, and her hair had grown even thicker and more lustrous. Her body had filled out to be that of a woman's; Mary marveled at it as though it were not her own.

But happy as Mary had been here, she was more than eager to start her journey home. Upon arrival, she would send word that she wanted to meet with Joseph, alone, in the olive orchard. He would know the place—it was where he had first professed out loud his love for her. And upon hearing his words, she had clapped her hands together in delight. May they share such joy again, Mary thought. May they once again regard their lives together as full of promise.

The traveler at the lead, a stout man with an immense beard, called out to Mary, and she strode forward, her steps light, her heart full of hope.

CHAPTER SEVEN

. . .

Nazareth

JUNE, 4 B.C.

Joseph

He sat with his back against the misshapen trunk of the olive tree. From far away, he saw her coming. He recognized the purposeful stride, the erect carriage, the proud lift of the head. He stood, reached behind to dust himself off, then straightened to the task at hand. He had walked here feeling sure of himself and of his decision, intractable in the words he meant to say. But now she came fully into view, and he found himself weakening. She had grown ripe and luscious, his Mary, who was no longer his. Gone suddenly was the righteous anger he had felt when Mary's mother had told him of the "angel" who had visited and made such an astonishing announcement. Gone the conviction that this would be a happy day, and that he would be better off without her, that indeed he had been lucky to have her terrible faults revealed before their wedding day.

His friends had told him she should be stoned as the adulteress that she was, and at first he had angrily agreed. She who questioned him unendingly, who made him feel foolish about beliefs he held, beliefs for which others praised him! She who had brazenly put her hand on his knee long before it was time for such things. He should have known then, he had told himself. On that very day, months ago, he should have divorced her, rather than having to face the humiliation brought by her coming back to their village with child. He had resolved to speak of the few things necessary and then leave. He would tell her that he would not have her stoned, but neither would he take her as his wife—he had prepared the document that released his rights over her. He would tell her of his great disappointment in her—let her for once not interrupt him!—his great disappointment, and his great sense of shame. He would tell her of all he had been made to endure while she so blithely went away to visit her relatives. The only one immediately kind to Joseph—apart from Mary's parents, and who welcomed their attention now?—had been Naomi. And Joseph had fully intended to tell Mary everything about Naomi. Her pride in the things women should take pride in, her proper disinterest in things not womanly. Her deference to him—not once had she questioned anything he had said. He had imagined, indeed hoped for, pain in Mary's face when he told her that Naomi was much better suited for the role of his wife, a role Mary obviously cared nothing about. He had decided that at the point when she covered her face in shame and wept, he would turn and walk away.

But there she was before him, her beauty more breathtaking than ever. She moved closer, and he smelled her sweet scent and saw her smile, and even while he told himself to step back, he moved forward. He caught her in his arms, buried his face in her neck, and began to weep.

"Joseph," she said softly. "Joseph. My beloved husband."

He pulled away from her angrily, wiped at his face, and felt his hands begin to tremble. At least part of his rage was directed against himself, for his weakness. "Do not call me husband, for such is not your privilege! You have disgraced and humiliated me! You have—"

"Have you not spoken with my mother?" Mary asked. "Did she not tell you the circumstances of my condition?"

"Mary. I shall ask you once and once only to hold your tongue. Hold your tongue! And listen to me! Show me at the ending of our union the respect you should have shown at the beginning!"

Her eyes filled with tears. "Why do you raise your voice against me? Your words do not hurt me more for being so loudly spoken."

He stood still, aware of the fact that he was panting. She was so beautiful. She could manipulate a weak man as easily as wet clay. But Joseph was not weak! He was strong! He spoke more quietly, saying, "I shall dispense with the things I deserve most wholeheartedly to say to you. Instead, I will tell you only this: We are divorced. I have prepared the document."

She spoke calmly. "Joseph. I am with child."

The words pierced him through, and for a moment he could not answer her. Finally, his mouth dry, he said, "As I am exceedingly well aware." He cast his eyes to the little mound of her belly. It looked dear to him, he realized; it moved him, and he looked quickly away. In a voice hard with pain, he said, "You are free to marry another." He felt hollow saying this; his eyes hung heavy in their sockets.

"Who would have me now? And Joseph, *Joseph,* I want no other man! I have come to understand your great worth, as well as the depth of my love for you. In my time away, I—"

He spoke over her as if he had not heard a word. "You are free to marry another, as am I. And I intend to take Naomi as my betrothed."

Mary turned quickly to look in the direction of their village, in the direction of Naomi's house. Her high forehead, her strong nose, her soft mouth! When she turned back to him, he did not see in her the pain he desired, or even anger. It was only Mary he saw, as he had always known her. Her clear eyes, her direct gaze. But still, that distance—she lived far behind her eyes.

"Have you love for Naomi?" she asked.

He opened his mouth to answer, then did not. He started to walk away.

"Joseph!" she called after him. "Do not turn away from me, who desires only to tell you the truth! Take me not as your wife, if that is your desire, but before you go, let me reveal to you all that is in my heart!"

He stood immobile. If she wanted to talk, let her come to him.

When Mary saw that he was waiting—though with his arms crossed over his chest and his face turned away—she moved closer to him. Her voice was low and rich, intimate, achingly familiar. "I know that my mother has told you of the angel's visit to me. And I know you find it hard to believe or understand. As I assure you I did also! I was terrified by his presence! But oh, Joseph, such rich understanding has come to me, such clarity of purpose, such joy at the change in me that causes you such pain! For I know with certainty that the Holy Spirit came unto me, and—"

"Blasphemy!"

She moved yet closer to him and gently put her hand on his arm. "Joseph. You of all people know and revere the power of God. If he chooses to visit a miracle upon us, who are we to question his methods? I tell you that I have been chosen to bring into the world the Son of God, and—"

Joseph yanked his arm from her. "I will hear no more!"

He strode quickly away.

He could feel her watching him go. And then she shouted after him, "Divorce me, then! And I divorce you also! For your great lack of faith, you who study the Torah! For your cowardice, you who call yourself strong!" Then, finally, she fell silent, and next he heard the loud sounds of weeping he had so desired but that now tore at his heart. He focused on the short sounds of his exhalations, the flapping of his sandals against the parched, unyielding earth. He walked more quickly, then ran, toward home.

Joseph tossed and turned on his pallet, unable to sleep. Just before dawn, he became aware of a presence beside him. He turned toward it. "Mother? . . . Father?"

There was no sound, but rather a throbbing silence. Then a voice said, "Joseph, son of David. Be not afraid to take Mary as your wife, for the child conceived in her is of the Holy Spirit. She will give birth to him, and he will be named Jesus, which means 'He who saves,' for he will deliver his people from their sins."

Joseph lay rigid, afraid to move, afraid to respond.

The voice continued, "All this was done to fulfill a prophecy that says, 'A virgin will be with child, and shall bring forth a son, and the people will call him Emmanuel, meaning 'God is with us.' "

Joseph swallowed, then slowly rose up on one elbow. He saw nothing. Heard nothing. He lay back down, his eyes wide, and then he bolted from his pallet.

The sky was tinged with pink by the time he arrived at Mary's house. The rooster strutted through the courtyard, ruffling his feathers and preening, preparing to announce the beginning of a new day.

Joseph stole into the house and went quietly over to Mary's pallet. He stooped down, whispered her name, and touched her lightly on the arm. She gasped and sat up, and Joseph held his finger to his lips. Fortunate now the age of Mary's parents and their poor hearing! He looked over to the other side of the room and saw Joachim snoring loudly, sleeping on his back with his limbs splayed. Anne faced the wall, curled up on her side, breathing deeply and regularly. Joseph smiled at Mary, but she did not return his smile. She sat still, staring at him.

He waved urgently toward himself for her to follow him. Still she sat. He mouthed, "Come with me!"

Gravely, she shook her head.

He looked quickly again at Mary's parents, then sat back on his heels and regarded her. A moment passed, then another. Then Joseph put his hands in the prayer position and entreated her with his eyes, and Mary finally stood and followed him out into the courtyard.

There she crossed her arms and said, "What business have you with me?"

"Mary," he said, "an angel has now come to me."

"Joseph!"

He put his finger to his lips. "Come with me." She stood still, breathless, then reached out eagerly for his hand. He closed his eyes in a brief moment of gratitude, then led her out toward the fields.

Once there, he bid her sit down, and he sat next to her. The day was glorious, still night-cool. Butterflies flew up and down and all around, huge white clouds drifted past, and wildflowers nodded in the breeze.

"Tell me of your angel," Mary said. "Of what did he speak?"

Joseph shrugged. "He? Or she? I know not which. Did you see your angel?"

"I saw mostly bright light, but also I saw the outline."

"I saw only darkness and heard a voice."

"But what did it say?"

He looked at her, his beauty, his flower. "First, I must confess . . . perhaps it did not truly happen."

She pulled back and frowned. "How do you mean this?"

"I mean that in my great weariness—for I slept not at all last night—I fear I heard things that were not there. Things that would have me not divorce you. For what the angel said is that I should not fear to take you as my wife. He said that the child in you has come to fulfill a prophecy, that you will give birth to one who saves his people from sin, and therefore he will be named—"

"Jesus," she said. They said it together.

"He said the child was conceived by the Holy Spirit."

Mary clapped her hands together and raised her eyes to the sky. "Then you believe! I thank God."

Joseph shook his head sadly. "Ah, Mary. What shall I make of these exotic fabulations? For, in truth, these things seem more fit for stories that children might tell than as direction for our lives. Are they dreams, these angels? A shared vision? Are they true? Are they false? Are they the miracles you and others say they are? Or are they Devil himself, come to dissuade good men from a righteous path? I tell you that by God, I know not. I know not!" He looked at her with great love and deep sadness. "I know nothing for certain but that my love for you abides. And so I shall take you unto me as my wife after all."

"Oh, Joseph! My heart is lifted up."

"But hear me now. We shall be married tomorrow, in secret. We shall have no feast to which we invite the village. It would not be proper."

Mary hung her head and nodded. One who did not know her as Joseph did might think she was disappointed. But Joseph knew she hung her head to hide her smile. It was Joseph's mother who would rend her garments and wail. But no matter his mother's tears; it would be with them as he had said. In the morning, in a small, legal ceremony, they would be wed.

For now, he stood and held out his hand to her.

"Where do we go now?" she asked.

"Ask no questions. Come."

She followed him back toward the village, then to one of the streets opposite the area where Mary lived. There, he pointed to a house at the end of a row of houses like it. But this one was obviously new; the white limestone shone hard in the sun. Trying to suppress his feeling of pride, he watched

Mary walk toward it. It was a fine structure, though he did say so himself! Two stories and four rooms, a large oven in the corner. Steps even and wide leading up to the roof, windows properly spaced high along the outside walls. Mary reached the door and stopped, then turned to Joseph, her face full of a pleasure so rich it looked like pain. He had carved birds into the door, hundreds of them. Some were aloft, some were nesting, some sat on branches in groups. And one, eye level with whomever came to the door, offered an olive branch.

He reached past her to open the door, and she went inside. After Joseph came in, she closed the door behind them and reached for him, putting her arms around his neck. But he stepped away from her, saying, "Not now, Mary. Nor tomorrow, nor the day after, nor the day after that. Only when it has left your body will I know you."

Mary moved her hand to her stomach and spread her fingers wide. "He is not an it."

Joseph shrugged. "For now, we shall go back to the houses of Anne and Joachim, and Rachel and Jacob, to tell them the news. We must not stay here; it is improper until we have had our wedding ceremony."

Mary looked around excitedly, then spoke, her voice earnest. "I honor this and all our traditions." She gestured for Joseph to go out before her, and took one last look around. Then she closed the door behind her gently, as though it might break. As though it had been crafted not from sturdy wood but from spun glass, and required great care in the handling.

She took his hand and walked closely beside him, and he looked down on her black hair, her perfect shoulders, the rise of her breasts grown larger with pregnancy. She moved with indescribable grace, and he thought of how he would lie with her someday. But not now. Not yet. Not until her womb was again empty and they were, in that way, back to where they'd started. And it was from there, he thought, that they would begin again.

On their wedding night Joseph lay on his side, turned away from Mary.

"Joseph?" she said.

"I am weary, my wife."

"Yet I am full of thoughts and so many feelings! Can we not speak? Have you no words at all for your wife on the day you have wed her?"

He turned to face her, suddenly shy. "Of what shall we speak?"

Mary smiled and reached out to run her fingers along the side of his face. Her touch! "I am happy to be here."

"And I am happy you are happy." He kissed her fingers and then took his hand away. No good would come of him being further aroused.

Mary took in a deep breath. "And I shall say, as well, that I hope you will come to see that what the angel told you—"

"We shall speak of it no more. I order this, my wife."

She lay quietly, then said, "Would you like to feel it?"

He knew what she meant. Her rounded stomach. "No," he said.

"He moves most actively this night. Perhaps he is telling us of his joy at our union."

"No, Mary." He yawned, though he felt no need to.

"Or perhaps he is frightened at his new

surroundings. Oh, Joseph. Do you think he is frightened?"

He made his breathing go deep and regular, that she might think him asleep. After a time, he heard her leave her pallet and move out to the other room. He rose and followed at a distance in the darkness. She wrapped a shawl around herself and slipped out the door. Was she leaving him? Again? He was ready to call out angrily to her when, through the crack in the door, he saw her sit with her back to the house and look up at the stars. She sang, softly, sweetly, and rocked herself from side to side. Both of her hands rested over her belly, and when she had finished singing she looked down at herself. "Shhhhh," she whispered. "I am here now as ever I shall be. Great is my love for you, and my devotion enough for two." Again she rocked from side to side, and the smile on her face Joseph felt in his knees.

CHAPTER EIGHT

. . .

Nazareth

DECEMBER, 4 B.C.

Joseph

He lagged, coming home. He dreaded sharing with his wife the news he'd learned at the marketplace. A census had been ordered by Caesar Augustus in Rome. A messenger, accompanied by Roman soldiers, had stood in the middle of the crowd to read: *I, King Herod, as a friend of Caesar, decree: Let every man repair to the place of origin of his house and family and have his name inscribed in the public registers.* After the soldier's departure, the Nazarenes had talked worriedly among themselves. Once their names were inscribed, they could no longer evade the payment of the poll tax.

Also, they would owe more taxes on their land, as it would now be more accurately assessed. Already they were poor and struggling; must they become poorer still?

Joseph put away the donkey in the workshop he had built next to the house; it doubled as a stable at night. He filled one bucket with grain and another with water. He spread hay for the animal's bed. "More troubles for we who are troubled, eh?" he said. The donkey stared at him and swished his tail. "I am as well without a solution," Joseph said. He patted the donkey's rump and went inside the house.

Mary was at the stove, stirring the chickpea-and-eggplant stew she had made. A fresh loaf of bread rested on top of the stove. She turned to greet him, flush-faced and happy. But her smiled faded when she saw him.

"What has happened?"

Joseph let himself down wearily into the chair he had made only last week. That was when he was feeling secure about his own success, sure that he would grow more and more prosperous and that soon he and Mary would have more chairs than they could use. Enough for the whole village! he had told her. "We shall offer to lend them to those having wedding feasts, that all their guests may sit in comfort." For it was indeed the season for weddings. With no seeds to sow, with no harvesting of barley and wheat and olives and grapes to consume entire days, young people had time to celebrate the end of their betrothals and the beginning of their married lives. Only last week, Mary and Joseph, along with their parents, had attended a lavish wedding. Rachel's eyes had filled with tears, watching the couple exchange vows, and Joseph had suspected it was not because of the usual poignancy attached to new love and the beginning of a new life. His suspicions were confirmed when, after consuming a large goblet of wine, she had collapsed into a chair, blubbering and saying over and over, "You would have had better." Jacob had apologetically escorted her away from the festivities.

Joseph had looked for signs of envy or regret in Mary and had found none. She was genuinely glad for the couple, and pleased with her own circumstances. For their life together was going well. They loved each other, they were content in their work, and their parents were looking forward to the coming of their grandchild—though each set of parents had their own ideas about the baby's origins. Rachel was markedly cool with Mary for over a month, and Jacob fearful of being too friendly. He liked Mary a great deal, but feared his wife more. Therefore he lowered his head when he welcomed Mary to his home and suppressed his normal jubilant self around her in deference to Rachel, who would not so much as offer Mary a smile. But that awkward time was gone now, and all waited in pleasant anticipation for the child, who was due soon. The midwife who met Mary at the well only last week had predicted three weeks more, and her predictions were remarkably accurate.

Now this. Now Joseph, born in Bethlehem, would need to make the long journey there. It was more than eighty miles and would take ten days, round-trip. But he must go. And so in answer to Mary's worried question about what had happened, he answered, "There has been a decree issued. All must register for a census in the town of their birth. Therefore we must go to Bethlehem."

"But I am so near my time!" Mary said.

Joseph shrugged. "Caesar cares not."

Mary moved to sit beside him. "I shall stay with my parents."

"No, Mary. As my wife, you will make the journey with me."

"I am near my time!" she said again, and again Joseph said, "Caesar cares not! We must leave in the morning, Mary. And now may I have my dinner?"

Mary looked into Joseph's face, weighing arguing with him, he knew. Then she went to the stove and filled two bowls with her stew, which was every bit as delicious as it smelled, and he told her so. After a long moment, she thanked him.

Later, when they lay on their pallets before sleep, he reached out to touch her shoulder. "I am sorry to ask this of you, my wife."

She turned toward him. "It is only that I fear for the child."

"You must not fear. For I will care for you both."

She drew in a quick breath. Then she nodded, patted Joseph's hand, and turned away from him. He sensed that her spirits had lifted markedly, for never had Joseph said he would care for the child. Never had he mentioned him.

"Do you smile in the darkness?" he asked.

Silence.

"Mary?"

She giggled, then turned back to him. She kissed his forehead, his eyes, his mouth. And then he kissed hers. It was their way.

"Our journey will go quickly," he said. "We will soon return, and then the baby will be born, and all will be well."

CHAPTER NINE

...

Bethlehem

DECEMBER 25

Mary

Shivering on the cold ground at night, her wool cloak her only covering. Covering her ears against the cries of leopards and jackals that lived in the brush of the Jordan River valley. During the day, dust in her nose, in her hair. The ever-growing soreness in her back, her buttocks, her legs. The terrible thirst—once, Mary nearly fainted for want of water. And once she nearly fell from the donkey when he stumbled on a rock. A near robbery, until Joseph talked his way out of it, saying that he had money only for a night's lodging in

Bethlehem, and could they not see how great with child his wife was?

"Would that you had let me stay with my parents," Mary had said bitterly, after the robbery attempt.

"Who then would have frightened the robbers away?" Joseph had turned from leading their donkey to grin at her. Finally, she returned the smile.

On the fifth day, as the sun was going down and the cold of the night again setting in, they reached the outskirts of Bethlehem. "We will first find lodging," Joseph said. "Then, early in the morning, we will register. And then we will begin our journey home."

Mary was worried. She had not told Joseph, for what, after all, could he do? It was a midwife she needed to talk to. Late that morning she had begun having pains. They were not the dull cramps she'd been feeling the last couple of weeks; these were harder. Yet they were not labor pains, either; of this she felt certain. She had seen women in labor, Elizabeth most recently, and these were not labor pains.

But then there came a sudden wetness

beneath her, and Mary knew well what it was. She put her hand to her stomach. "Joseph?"

"Yes?" He turned to look back at her. In his face was great weariness. The journey had been hard on him, too; the last few miles, he had leaned heavily on his walking staff. "What is it?"

She swallowed.

Joseph's eyes grew wide. He halted the donkey and asked anxiously, "Are you . . . ? Oh, Mary, is it time?"

She nodded.

He stood stock-still. Clasped his hand together tightly. Leaned over to embrace her. Clasped his hands together again. Drew himself up and attempted, unsuccessfully, to speak slowly. "We shall find lodging and a midwife. Can you wait?"

She smiled at him, in spite of herself.

"Oh, I . . . forgive me, I know, I . . ." He kissed her forehead, her eyes, her mouth, and moved to lead the donkey forward. "Do not worry!" he called back to her.

But she was worried.

• • •

More than three hours later, they had found nothing. Every inn was filled; people who had come to register had taken all the rooms. And though she knew it was not Joseph's fault, though she knew he was doing all he could to find a place for them, Mary unleashed her fury upon him.

"You should not have had me come!" she said. "Because of you, my child is threatened—and myself, as well! I am in *agony,* and I must ride endlessly on a *donkey,* in search of something we cannot *find*!"

To all this, Joseph said nothing. He guided the donkey along, trying to keep him from going too fast and increasing her discomfort. It was not easy. Once, startled by something he saw, the donkey broke into a trot. Mary cried out, and in frustration Joseph jerked on the donkey's lead and slapped him across the nose. The animal reared his head back and brayed. Joseph rushed to Mary's side. "Are you all right?"

And she struck Joseph's shoulder, saying, "Do not strike the *donkey*!" Then she put her face in her hands and began to weep.

Joseph stood still on the narrow street.

"Mary," he said. "I know not what to do. Forgive me."

Mary continued to weep, and Joseph stood before her, his hands at his side, his face full of anguish. "Forgive me," he said again. Then he gently touched her knee and moved back to the donkey. "I shall ask forgiveness of you as well," he said, and pulled at the lead to turn the beast around.

"Where are we going?" Mary asked, panic in her voice. Was he going back to Nazareth? They could not! For now her labor had become intense; wave after wave of excruciating pain bore down upon her. She felt sick to her stomach; she needed to lie down.

"We will go back to the last inn," Joseph said. "I will insist that he give us a room! I will tell him we can share with others."

Mary drew in a deep breath and held on. The last inn they'd been to was not far. She thought she could make it.

When they arrived, Joseph left Mary in the street and ran to the door. She saw him gesture animatedly to the innkeeper; she saw the innkeeper shake his head. Joseph pointed to her, and the innkeeper peered around Joseph to look at her and shrugged.

He lifted his hands in a gesture of helplessness. Joseph raised his voice so that Mary could hear him plainly. "I tell you she is going to give birth! Now!"

From behind the innkeeper, Mary saw a woman's head peeking out. Then she squeezed past and stood before him, hands on her hips, looking out at Mary. She spoke to her husband in low tones, and again he shook his head. She said something else, more sharply, and he shrugged, then walked away.

Joseph ran back to Mary. "What did they say?" she asked, full of hope.

"They have a stable. It is next to the inn, out of the cold."

"A stable?"

"Next to the inn. There is an empty stall." He began leading the donkey forward.

"A stable? I am to give birth in a *stable*?" Where would the hot water come from? Where the clean white cloths? Where the midwife's stone, so that she could sit properly between Mary's legs, and where the midwife's assistants to hold Mary in such a way that she might better push? From where would come the aromatic oils to massage into her temples, the giant fennel to speed the labor, the sawdust to soak up the blood? There would be no women's voices soothing her during her labor, no jubilant ululating after the birth, no feast offered to the newly delivered mother. She had nothing but Joseph.

And now not even him, for he lifted her off the donkey, helped her to lie down, and then said, "Wait for me here. They have told me where I might find a midwife."

"Joseph!" she said. "Do not leave me! The baby is coming!"

"I shall be back as soon as I can. Mary, I must find a midwife. I know not what to do!"

He ran into the night. Dazed, Mary lay with her hands over her fiercely contracting stomach. A clucking chicken walked across her ankles, and its sharp claws cut her. The donkey was tethered beside a mule, and they both regarded her with a placid curiosity. There were two sheep, one baaing continuously. A rat ran across a corner of the stable and disappeared into the hay.

"Mother!" Mary wailed, then cried for Anne yet again.

Then she grew silent. There was no use in wasting her energy this way. The baby was coming, no matter where she lay. She would need to pay attention and help herself, for surely the midwife would arrive too late.

She rose with difficulty and replaced the soiled hay beneath her with clean. Then she lay back down and took in long, deep breaths, trying to calm herself the way she had seen Elizabeth do. She closed her eyes and massaged her temples. She looked about for something to use as a holding rope, something that she might pull on with the pain, but saw nothing. So she removed her head cover and tied one end to the leg of the nearby manger. She tested it, pulling on it. And then used it for its purpose, as a hard pain came upon her. She rose up, clenched her teeth and pulled on the rope, clenched her teeth harder and pulled again. When the pain subsided, she lay back down and allowed herself one more moment of pity for her poor circumstances: She lay on the floor of a stranger's stable. Somewhere, water dripped. The air was foul with the scent of the animals and their droppings. Wind blew in through the cracks of the walls. She closed her eyes. So be it.

When the next pain came, she rose again and pulled.

And then Joseph and a young girl came hurrying through the stable door toward her. Mary smiled, then wept with relief. The girl pushed up Mary's tunic, parted her legs, and gasped. Then, "Push!" she said.

Mary pushed, then said politely, "I am Mary of Nazareth."

The girl spoke rapidly. "I am but a shepherdess, only two months ago having given birth myself. Thus has your husband asked me to help you. But I am only a shepherdess."

Mary pushed again. "What is your name?"

"I am Rebecca of Bethlehem." The girl was dirty-faced and looked full of fear; surely she was worried about failing these strangers, about being blamed if the baby or the mother died.

"I am grateful for your presence," Mary said, then spoke no more.

She endured massive waves of pain, and in between them pushed with all her might. Joseph sat crouched near the doorway, helpless, his eyes wide. Mary looked at him and then beyond him, at the black sky filled with stars—she had never seen such stars. There was one far brighter than the others, and it was this star that she eventually focused on, for its ethereal presence brought her calm.

There came a sudden darkness, and Joseph, alarmed, stood and looked up at the sky. Mary rose to her elbows. But then as quickly as the dark had come, there came a blinding light from inside the stable. Joseph closed his eyes against it, and when he opened them again, the baby had been born.

Mary sat with her back against a bale of hay, holding Jesus. He had not yet cried, not even when he slipped out of her warm body and into the coldness of the night. He lay open-eyed and calm in her arms, and she stared down into his face, calm herself. Joseph sat beside her, wordless with gratitude that his wife had survived. He looked at her with the same adoration that shone on Mary's face.

As soon as the shepherd girl had delivered the baby—a slight rotation of the

shoulders was all that had been needed—
she had run for supplies she'd not had time
to fetch before. Now she returned with rags
to clean Mary and the baby, and from
which to make swaddling clothes. "He is a
fine baby!" she told Mary, as she tore long
strips from a tunic. "He has the same well-
formed head as did my own Isaiah." She
smiled, her face full of pride at the thought
of her son.

"Is he your first?" Mary asked, and
Rebecca smiled and nodded. "But I pray
that there will be many more, now that I have
seen what endless joy comes to those with
children."

Behind Rebecca were two of the shepherds who had come down from the hills.
They stood far back, speaking quietly to
each other and craning their necks, trying
to see the baby.

When she and Rebecca had finished
swaddling him, Mary lay her son in the
manger, which had been filled with clean,
sweet-smelling hay. "You may come closer,
and see him," she told the shepherds. The
men exchanged glances, one scratching
absentmindedly at his chest, then under
his arm. But then they approached, their

hands at their sides, their faces full of humility and the kind of wonder always seen after a birth. But more. For one of the men, upon seeing the infant, fell to his knees. The second man quickly followed. Joseph looked over at Mary. She smiled.

The next evening Rebecca returned to cut the cord. The baby had had a full day to draw on the powers of the placenta, and now it was time for him to be separated from it. Mary regretted that the placenta would be buried here, without the embroidered bag she had made to hold it. That bag lay beside the chair in her kitchen, at home. She would save it for the next baby, for according to Joseph's plan, there would be many more.

When Rebecca had finished and was ready to go, Mary took the young girl's hands into her own and thanked her. She bid Joseph give Rebecca part of what they had intended to pay the innkeeper. Joseph gave her this, as well as figs and lentils from the little food they had remaining.

Rebecca, blushing, thanked them again

and again. Then she said, "It seems the birth of your child is most auspicious. Last night, after my leave-taking to come and assist you, the other shepherds were sleeping in the fields with the flocks when an angel suddenly appeared! They described it as glorious in appearance, bright unto blinding. At first they were afraid, and they banded together that their nearness to one another might offer comfort. But then the angel spoke, telling them not to be afraid, telling them that he brought great tidings of joy. He said that in Bethlehem, the city of David, a savior had been born unto them and indeed unto all people. And he said there would be a sign: that the child would be in a manger, dressed in swaddling clothes. Then there appeared alongside the angel a great multitude. And they said, 'Glory to God in the highest, and on earth peace, goodwill toward men.' Therefore those two came down from the hills into Bethlehem, that they might see. Indeed the word has spread, and I know of many more who intend to come." Rebecca stood staring, waiting, it seemed, for Mary and Joseph to confirm the truth of all this.

Mary held her baby closer and looked to

Joseph to answer. It was his place. But he only smiled at Rebecca and thanked her again for her help. Then he spoke to Mary, saying, "The baby must be circumcised and named on the eighth day. In the morning, we will go to Jerusalem for that purpose." His jaw tightened. "And then we will return home to await the time of your purification."

As soon as the sun rose the next morning, Mary and Joseph began another journey, the three of them now. It was only eight miles to Jerusalem, and so the trip would be far less arduous than their last had been, on all counts. Joseph had told Mary they had enough money to stay at an inn in Jerusalem, and she relished the thought of such luxury.

When they were outside Bethlehem and alone on the road, Mary said, "Tell me of your thoughts, Joseph." She knew he had been bothered by the idea of so many strangers talking about the baby's birth, by so many people wanting to see him. It was for this reason, she felt sure, that they had journeyed to another place to await the circumcision.

For a long while, Joseph did not answer

Mary. She stared at his straight back, leading the donkey forward. Finally, he turned to her and said, "We shall find the wisest elder in the city to attend to our son." A great love for Joseph rose up in Mary, but she did not speak. She nodded, and Joseph nodded back. Then he turned to urge the donkey forward again. "I grow hungry," he said. "Soon we shall stop to eat."

The city was dense with people and activities, but this held no allure for either of them. They were weary, and Mary was sore from the ride. They moved in silence through the loud crowds and bore the constant jostling, which was at times extreme. One young man lost his balance and fell at Joseph's feet; then, rolling out of the way, he narrowly missed the hooves of the donkey. Joseph found an inn near the outskirts of the city, and that night they all slept so soundly that the innkeeper banged at the door in the late morning, fearful that they had died or escaped without paying.

They passed the days until the circumcision strolling about the city, talking quietly about their life back in Nazareth, about how, with the addition of the baby, it was forever changed. They ate little, for their money was almost gone, and Mary spoke often of how they would feast once they were back home. They spoke, too, of how odd it was to see so many strangers, and never the same face twice. In their town, every face was known to them.

On the morning of the eighth day, Mary washed and swaddled Jesus and then handed him to Joseph. As childbirth was woman's province, circumcision was man's. Joseph would bring the baby to the village elder they had decided upon, who would pull the baby's flesh tight and cut quickly, then apply a dressing of wine and olive oil with balm and cumin. Tears fell from Mary's eyes, and she quickly wiped them away.

"This is a moment to be proud!" Joseph said. "It is his first act of manhood!"

"But unfortunate for the way that pain must accompany it," she said. "I shall await his other acts of manhood, which will bring only joy to him and to us."

As Joseph was walking out, Mary said, "Remember, as soon as you are finished, we will start for home. And go first to my parents' house."

"Yes, yes, I remember," Joseph said. He was right to be impatient; Mary had reminded him of this several times during their stay in Jerusalem. Also she had imagined aloud a thousand times the love and wonder in Anne's and Joachim's faces when they first looked upon their grandchild. And the pride they would have in her. And Joseph! she hastily added, but at this his face remained empty of emotion.

CHAPTER TEN

. . .

Nazareth
JANUARY, 3 B.C.

Joseph

"He is called Jesus," Mary said. It was late afternoon and she was sitting in the house of Anne and Joachim. Her parents stood before her, bent down to admire the baby. Joseph had kept himself out of the way so that Mary's parents might better see their child's child: his well-formed head, his sturdy body, his arresting calm. Joseph was eager to return home, for he was greatly weary, but he owed his wife time with her mother and father.

He gazed at her now, smiling up at her parents, her skin bruised-looking beneath her eyes. He regretted all she had been through and admitted to himself that perhaps she should not have accompanied him after all. She could have stayed with her parents and had the assistance to which she was entitled when it came time to give birth. One from their own village could have performed the circumcision. And the baby's birth surely would not have drawn so much attention. Joseph had spoken to Mary of her wifely duty to accompany him to Bethlehem, but he wondered now if he had simply not trusted her being without him.

Yet he did not doubt her love for him. She showed him in so many ways that she was content with him, honored to be his chosen one. She kept the house well, she cooked with great skill and pleasure; she seemed eager to raise children with him. Often she spoke of names that might be used for the children yet to come, of games they might play with them, of the many things they and their grandparents might teach them. She spoke most winningly of how the love they had for each other would grow and include the children, how *family* would displace *couple* in ways marvelous and satisfying. Yet there was always her odd separateness, her distance from him. Often he asked her, as he had on the day he met her, where she was from; and behind his teasing, there was a kind of serious inquiry. Always she laughed at him, and made up different answers for his amusement. "I come from the moon," she had said once, as they sat out in the courtyard admiring the stars. "From the depths of the ocean," she said another time. And once, she had looked deep into his eyes and said, "I come from your imagination. I am not really here." He had reached out to hold her. "What accounts then for this warmth I feel?" he had asked. "From what part of my mind comes this sweet perfume? Or the silkiness of this hair, or the softness of these lips?" And then they had spoken no more, until his arousal had made him go outside to walk for relief.

But after Mary's purification, which was soon to come, he would no longer need to hold back the expression of his affection. The sudden rush of joy he felt at this thought made his fatigue all but disappear. Still, he finally told Mary, "We must go now; we are all weary and I desire that we take our rest in our own house, at long last."

Anne rose from where she had knelt beside Mary to gently caress the child's forehead. Jesus lay silent, his eyes wide, regarding all that lay about him. The baby cried rarely: only to show his want for food. Joseph felt a reluctant pride in him, and his heart twisted as he imagined Mary's did when the child's face crumpled and his wails pierced the air. Of course Joseph did not show his wife such unseemly vulnerability. On their journey home, whenever Jesus cried, Joseph had said only, "Shall I stop that you might feed him?" He had kept his voice strong and neutral, and he had not stared too long when the baby was at her breast. But already he loved the child. Already, he had imagined holding his own hand over the boy's a few years from now, showing him how to plane boards or set stone. Already he had imagined his son learning more rapidly, more thoroughly, than the other boys at synagogue. He had even imagined himself at his son's wedding, dancing with Mary while Jesus danced with his bride.

"Of course you must go now," Anne said. "Soon it will be night. You must all take your rest. Take with you this bread I have baked, and take too some cheese and apricots. And tomorrow, come for Sabbath dinner. I shall roast a lamb."

Mary and Joseph embraced her parents. Then Anne and Joachim followed the couple out to the courtyard, and Anne told Joachim to go for more olive oil. "Do not tarry," she told him. "I have much to do to prepare for our celebration tomorrow. And go also to the house of Rachel and Jacob; invite them to come as well."

From across the courtyard, a neighbor called out to Joachim. He was pulling behind him a listless goat. The animal took a step and hesitated, took another and lay down. "Speak with my husband later!" Anne called out, but it was useless; already Joachim had knelt down and put his hand to the animal's head and was speaking softly to it. Anne crossed her arms and shook her head, but she was smiling. She waved her hand in dismissal and went back inside.

CHAPTER ELEVEN

. . .

Jerusalem

FEBRUARY, 3 B.C.

Joseph

The laws in Leviticus dictated that a woman
was to be purified thirty-three days after her
son's circumcision. The night before
Joseph and Mary were to begin the journey
to Jerusalem for that purpose, Joseph lay
wide awake on his pallet.

In keeping with tradition, he would bring
Mary to the temple. There, they would
make an offering to the priest for a sacrifice
that would recognize God's sovereignty
and express gratitude for a healthy delivery.
Mary would enter the mikvah, the ritual
bath required of any woman who had given
birth. Three times, she would immerse her-

self in shoulder-high rain or spring water, reciting blessings. Joseph imagined her dark hair floating about her as she lowered herself beneath the surface of the water, then flattening against her back when she rose up. He saw her emerging from the pool and being wrapped by the attendant in a white flax towel. He saw her face lifted in joy as she was pronounced clean. It was what he had so longed for, this purification ceremony, because it would give him his wife as she should be. But now he felt a terrible uncertainty.

Mary had never deviated in any way from what she had told him about the angel's visit to her and her pregnancy—not with her voice, not with her eyes, not in her demeanor. When she slept, she was soundless, her face as blankly innocent as a child's. She *was* innocent, if you were to believe her. Odd, then, that she accepted as a matter of course—indeed accepted without question or comment—entering the living waters of the mikvah to be cleansed in the same way as women who had lain with men.

He rose up on one elbow and turned toward Mary, watching her sleep by the thin light of the moon. She lay on her side, her hands open and relaxed. Her breathing was deep and even, her brow smooth as marble. He touched her shoulder. Her breathing altered just slightly, then returned again to normal. As for the baby, Jesus, he too was awake. Calm and utterly silent in Mary's arms, he turned now to regard Joseph.

Joseph stared into the infant's eyes for a long moment. Then he lay flat on his back, sighed quietly, and slept.

Mary and Joseph arrived at the temple in the late morning, after having traveled the short distance from the village where they had spent the night before. At the north gate, Joseph presented the priest their offering for the sacrifice: two pigeons, a poor man's substitute for the preferred lamb and turtledove. Even so, Joseph had paid a handsome price for the birds; the vendors near the temple took advantage of the fact that pilgrims relied on them to sell unblemished animals that the priest would accept. Joseph had brought from home his

own grain and wine to be added to the offering.

As her baby slept soundly in Mary's arms,
she and Joseph moved to the south gate
of the temple, where for some time they
stood wordless, looking up at the grand
structure—with its plazas and immensely
long porticos, it occupied some thirty-five
acres. At the center was the white marble sanctuary and its altar of gold. No one
could go to the innermost room but the
high priest, and he himself went only
one day a year, on the Day of Atonement.

Joseph shook his head slowly as he
looked about. Here in this most magnificent
place were priests descended from Aaron
in the time of Moses. He suppressed a
tremble; the *sacredness*! It seemed held in
the very air around them—he could feel it,
almost hear it, and it created in him a deep
longing that brought tears to his eyes.
Quickly, he took Mary's arm to lead her up
the wide stairs and into the courtyard where
they would conduct their business: Mary
would be purified, and the child officially
presented to God. And then they would
journey back to Nazareth, and begin at last
to live a normal life.

• • •

When their obligations were fulfilled, Joseph drew himself up happily. "And now let us finally go home."

Mary walked quickly beside him, her footsteps echoing on the floor. She laughed out loud, then asked, "Do you remember, my husband, when I longed so to live in the city?"

He looked at her, one eyebrow raised. "I do."

"Never has our quiet village seemed more attractive! I now appreciate everything about it: the beauty of the green hills, the purity and abundance of the water from the spring, the rows of vines in my father's vineyard."

"The quiet!" Joseph said.

"Yes. The quiet also, that lets us hear the birds in the air and the sheep in the pastures. And I understand as well the value of the simplicity of our life. I love my friends and relatives. In Nazareth, I know everyone."

"I suppose you will be disappointed, then, when I tell you I have found work in Jerusalem," Joseph said.

She stopped walking and turned to him.

"I shall work on the temple, but only for fifty years or so."

She realized then his joking, and smiled at him. "Let us go home."

As they were nearing the staircase, they were accosted by an old man who appeared from around a corner. He took Jesus from Mary's arms, looked heavenward, and exclaimed, "Bless you, Lord! For now I may die in peace, according to your word." To the startled Joseph and Mary, he said, "I am Simeon, told that I would not see death until I had seen the Lord's Christ. The spirit has today brought me to the temple, and the prophecy has been fulfilled." He stared in the baby's face, saying, "Now you are here, and I have seen the salvation you have brought us all: a light of revelation to the Gentiles, and glory to your people, Israel." The man's arms trembled. His face was more bone than flesh. His ears were huge, false-looking in their enormity, and his tangled white eyebrows jutted forth from his face over his faded blue eyes.

And then there came the high, shrill voice of an ancient, bow-backed woman who limped forward, crying, "Now is here the redemption of Israel!" She sounded to Mary like crows cawing in the field, fighting over corn. The woman's head cover rode low over her forehead, shadowing her deep-set eyes. Her fingers were twisted and her knuckles swollen. Her mouth sank inward; she had no teeth.

Mary looked at Joseph. She seemed to be asking whether these were holy people or the town's lunatics. But he struggled to keep his face calm and accepting so that Mary would not be afraid.

"It is so, Anna," Simeon said to the old woman. "Rejoice, for it is so." He looked deeply into Mary's eyes. "You see that the prophetess who never leaves the temple, but prays here day and night, has also seen and made her pronouncement. Bless you! Your child is destined for the fall and the rising again of many in Israel. But he is a sign that will be spoken against, because he will cause the thoughts of many hearts to be revealed. A sword will pierce your soul, also."

Mary snatched Jesus back into her arms, startling him; his small arms flew up into the air. She drew her baby closer to her and spoke loudly to the man. "What is it you

mean to say? What are these strange pro-
nouncements?"

Joseph moved closer to Mary, put his
arm about her, and began to lead her out.
"Pay them no mind," he said.

Mary looked back over her shoulder at
the two old people who stood together,
watching them leave the temple.

"But did you hear their words, Joseph?
What do they mean?"

"They are old," he said simply. He helped
her onto the donkey. "And we are going
home to Nazareth, where we will now raise
this child, and many others, in peace."

But as he led the donkey once again
down the road, he turned over and over in
his mind the possible meaning of the many
strange words spoken to them since Jesus'
birth. The shepherd girl, with her talk of
Jesus being a savior, her story of angels
coming to the shepherds in their fields on
the night of his birth. The rumors of the
many others in Jerusalem who had spoken
about the birth, and of the people who were
journeying to see the baby. And now these
two old people at the temple. Some might
disregard the words of a simple shepherdess, but Joseph had felt the weight of

her words in his heart. And a prophet and prophetess, who said these things in the temple in Jerusalem! Joseph had told Mary to disregard them, but he could not quite convince himself of what he said to her with such confidence.

On the first night of their journey home, he lay awake beside Mary, listening to the cries of wild animals and the wind. But most of all, he listened to the chatter of his own mind, which demanded a rational explanation for all the events that had befallen them. About Mary's pregnancy, he had his own ideas. As for the rest, he was confounded by it.

CHAPTER TWELVE

. . .

Nazareth

Joseph

When Mary and Joseph had arrived back in Nazareth and were nearing their own house, a group of children came running toward them. "They want to see the baby," Mary said, smiling, and she began loosening the clothes around the baby's face. But the children did not want to see the baby; rather they wanted to tell Mary and Joseph that there were strangers waiting for them. Men from the city called Saba in Persia, wearing fine robes! And hats! And rings! They had followed a star, they'd said, that had stopped here, directly over the house of Mary and Joseph. They had brought gifts for the baby. Could they see? the children asked. Could they see what the men had brought?

Joseph kindly waved the children away, saying that they should come back tomorrow. Then he drew himself up and walked toward the house, pulling hard on the donkey's lead to make him move more quickly. He strained to see in the gathering darkness who was at their door.

There were three camels kneeling in the dirt outside Mary and Joseph's house. They wore bridles decorated with silver and gold, with tassels and bells; and the camels' saddles, resting on top of ornate rugs, were heavily loaded. Beside the camels sat three men, dressed in fine, heavy robes of purple and blue. One man was young and beardless, stout and ruddy-complected; one was an ancient white-haired man with a long beard that flowed halfway down his chest; the third was black-skinned and so tall he would need to bend, should he come into the house. They wore caps, as the children had said, and Joseph saw on their hands the many rings, as the children had also described—gold, with large stones of red, green, white, and blue. Also, the men wore multiple gold bracelets that jingled musically as they stood to greet the couple and their baby.

Joseph took the last few steps toward them warily. He helped Mary off the donkey and bid her go inside. She hesitated, but did as he had asked. He closed the door tightly behind her, then turned to face the men and asked, "Why are you come here?" His voice betrayed his nervousness, and he drew in a deep breath, that he might calm himself.

The old man spoke first. "I am Melchior," he said. His voice was dry, parched-sounding. He pointed to the black man. "And this is Balthasar."

The black man put his hands together under his chin and bowed. In one of his earlobes, a ruby sparkled. He spoke in a low voice and with an accent Joseph could not identify. "I bring you greetings and salutations."

Joseph said nothing. The old man pointed to the younger man. "This one is Gaspar."

"We have traveled long to see you!" Gaspar said. "We are come to see the child born unto your wife, for he is the King of the Jews!"

"Who has told you this?" Joseph asked irritably. Again these strange assertions!

Melchior raised his eyebrows and nodded slowly. "We are acquainted with exiled Jewish priests who live among us, and we know well of the prophecy: the birth of the Christ child. We have followed the star."

Gaspar spoke again. "It is the messianic star!" He pointed to the sky. "Look, you can see it hovering there. On the night of your child's birth, Jupiter, which represents kingship of the world, and Saturn, which is associated with Palestine, came close together in the constellation Pisces. This accounted for that most unusual brilliance. And when such an event occurs, it signals the birth of someone great."

"We traveled first to Jerusalem," said Melchior. "There we asked the people, 'Where is he that is born King of the Jews?' We told them that we had seen his star in the east and had followed it, that we might find the babe and worship him."

Balthasar continued, "Hearing of this,

Herod called for his chief priests and his scribes, asking where this child was to be born. They told him of this same prophecy, that from Bethlehem in Judea would come a ruler who would be shepherd to the people of Israel."

Gaspar spoke more quietly now. "Herod called to meet with us secretly so that he might learn the time the star had appeared. When we told him, he bid us find the child and report back to him, that he might come to worship him as well. But we are come to tell you grave news!" He ceased talking when the black man turned to look reproachfully at him.

"You must be frightened by our appearance," Balthasar told Joseph, "and more so by our eager companion's revelations. But we are here only to pay our respects to the Christ child, and to offer gifts."

"But how do you come to believe all this of the infant?" Joseph asked. "By what means do you arrive at this fantastic conclusion?"

Balthasar answered him. "As we have explained, it is the prophecy, which is well known to many. Moreover, we are skilled in dream interpretation and at divining both the past and the future. Gaspar is also an astronomer and a mathematician."

"Herod means to kill your son," Gaspar said, and this time he was not rebuked.

Joseph looked into their faces, one at a time. "Come inside," he said.

They found Mary just inside the door, holding Jesus. When the wise men saw the baby, they fell to their knees. Bewildered, Mary looked to Joseph.

"They are wise men," he told her.

She nodded, her eyes wide.

Inside the house, Joseph could smell the visitors; mixed in with the scent of camels and the dust of travel was an exotic fragrance, like a rare perfume. The men exuded a kind of power but also a great gentleness—even the loud one, Gaspar.

The men rose, and Balthasar pulled from his robe a velvet sack. He opened it and spilled out onto the earthen floor many pieces of gold. "That you may have enough for your journey, for you must escape from here."

Mary stepped back, startled, but Joseph felt rooted to the spot.

Melchior showed them his offering of frankincense, and Gaspar his of myrrh.

"Myrrh!" Mary said, and Gaspar spoke quickly, saying that in addition to being used to anoint the dead, myrrh might also be used as a painkiller.

"We cannot accept these gifts," Joseph said.

"We cannot," Mary echoed.

"We bid you take them," Balthasar said. "We have journeyed far to give them to you." He looked at Jesus, lying still in his mother's arms. "Blessings be upon him," he said. He moved one step closer, then another. Mary stood still, but her arms tightened around Jesus.

Balthasar stopped and held up his hand. "I shall come no closer. I mean only to admire the gift you have brought forth into the world."

Now Mary softened, and tilted the baby slightly toward him.

Joseph stood watching, wondering if this were a dream. He had heard of wise men from the east, but that they were here in Nazareth! Come to visit them!

Everything about these men was different: their dress, their speech, their movements and ways of speaking. They were like the very wealthy people Joseph sometimes saw in Sepphoris, who were *separate* by virtue of their station, by their very being. Yet these men were more exotic still. It was as though if he were to reach out and touch them, they still would not be touched. Looking at them, he could almost hear a strange kind of music, winding and enticing. They did not belong here in this humble village they had journeyed so far to find. Joseph tried to imagine how they traveled, where they stayed, to whom they spoke along the way. How many people now knew of the birth of Jesus? What could it mean?

Had Mary brought all of this on them, with her strange yearnings and desires, with her dreamy discontent? Why could she not be more like a normal girl, content to sit in the courtyard or go to the well with her mother and her friends, content to gossip and laugh and care for her family, to attend weddings and funerals and help with the harvests? Most important, why could she not have been pregnant at the proper time by the proper person? Ever since she had come back to Nazareth as an unwed mother, his world had been turned upside down. Would these odd and difficult occurrences never end? Would he and Mary never enjoy the life he had wanted for them, a life that would properly emulate that of their parents?

The three wise men had gathered now around Mary and Jesus, and they gazed with adoration at the baby. It was enough! He would no longer cooperate with the strange things being thrust upon him. This was his house, and he was the master of his own house! "I fear your presence here may attract unwanted attention," he said. "I must ask that you leave now."

They all turned to him, the men and Mary. Then Balthasar said quietly, "Yet you were already in danger, without us. I tell you once more, we are come only to pay our respects." He stepped back from Mary and nodded to the other two men. "But we shall go. For we ourselves must also flee Herod."

Gaspar said, "We were warned in a dream not to go back to Jerusalem but to return home by a different route."

Joseph put the gold back in the sack and

held it and the other two sacks out to the men. "I shall ask you again to take back your gifts."

None of them moved to take the sacks. Finally, Melchior said, "Peace be with you," and they bowed and departed.

Mary and Joseph stood at the door and watched them mount their camels. On a command from one of the men, the camels rose, and then the men headed off into the night, their heads bobbing from side to side in their slow ride. Joseph could hear the bells on the camels fade away until they could be heard no more. He closed the door, dropped the sacks onto the floor, and turned to Mary. "We shall not go."

She began to weep, and Joseph did not know if it was from fear or joy.

"We shall stay here in our home," he said, hesitantly now.

"Oh, Joseph," she said. "I am so relieved to hear you speak those words! It is well known that the wise men have supernatural vision and that their words must not be taken lightly. Yet even more than their warnings, I fear leaving here again."

"Come," Joseph said. He helped Mary to lie down on her pallet, Jesus in her arms.

"Too many strange things have happened!" Mary said. "I want only to raise my child in peace!"

Joseph closed his eyes in gladness to hear her say such things. "And you will," he said. "Rest now, we are home."

He sat beside her, stroking her hair and waiting for her to fall asleep. Then he crept quietly from the house to go to the well for water to fill the cistern, that they might have what they needed in the morning.

When he returned from his walk through the silent village, he lay beside Mary, who slept deeply. He thought of all that had come to pass since they journeyed to Bethlehem. He looked about his house, gratified to be inside its familiar walls. In a few days he would be back at work erecting fine buildings and then coming home to his family. He closed his eyes and slept.

In the middle of the night, Joseph awakened in a panic. He shook his wife's shoulder. "Mary! Awake and arise! We must go to Egypt!"

"Joseph?" she said sleepily.

He stood and pulled at her arm. "Arise, quickly! We must leave now!"

She sat up, confused, the child asleep in her arms. She spoke in a whisper. "Joseph! Awaken yourself; I fear you are dreaming! Joseph! Are you awake?"

He knelt down beside her. "Mary, I have had a most vivid dream of warning!" He did not want to tell her what he had seen in his dream: babies being slaughtered by the hundreds. "I have been instructed to go to Egypt."

"Egypt!"

"Yes, and we must leave immediately." He rose and began gathering items for their journey. Things only just unpacked were now tossed again into sacks. He packed bread, cheese, olives, nuts, and oranges. He filled one goatskin with water, then another. "Make haste!" he told Mary, who sat unmoving on her pallet.

"I shall not go with you," she said.

He stiffened. "Do not argue with me."

She began to weep. "We must cross the Sinai to get to Egypt! You yourself have told me no one crosses the Sinai without an army or at least a caravan. And it is night, besides!"

He tried to make himself sound calm and reasonable. "I cannot say strongly enough the urgency with which we must attend to this. The child's life is in danger. We must go. Now."

"Because of a *dream*?"

He spoke with his back to her as he packed the gifts the wise men had given them.

"It was an angel who came in the dream. An angel who spoke to me."

"Now you believe in an angel's words!" She rose slowly. "Yes, do not neglect to pack the myrrh we were given. For someone will surely have need of it to anoint us all!"

He did not answer but went to the work shed for the donkey, who, upon seeing him, rose immediately to his feet. "Good and faithful donkey," he said, "would that you might endow my wife with your same worthy qualities."

After he loaded up the donkey, he led it to the doorway of the house and called softly for Mary to come out. She closed the door behind her, then said, "Before we leave, I shall go to the house of my parents and bid them goodbye."

"The hour is late, Mary. They are sleeping."

She stood unmoving for a long time, until Joseph hung his head in resignation. Then she walked ahead of him and did not look back, nor did she look at him when he helped her mount the donkey outside her parents' house. "I shall never see my mother again," she said, and he knew she spoke truly. Mary made such predictions rarely; but when she did, she was never wrong.

Anne came outside and kissed Joseph after Mary had said goodbye, bidding him to travel safely and care well for her daughter and grandson. "Trust in her and in the love you share," she said. Then she stepped back, clasped her hands before her, and looked long upon Mary, and Joseph saw that Anne, too, knew that they would not see each other again.

Joachim stood smiling, putting up a brave front that fooled no one, and only when he thought Mary and Joseph had turned back for the last time did he wipe the tears from his face. But Joseph did turn back, and he nodded once at Joachim, who nodded in return. Then Joachim turned and walked slowly with Anne back into the house.

They had been in Egypt but a short time when they heard of Anne's death. Mary bore her pain quietly and, to Joseph's great relief, did not turn from him. Well over a year later, they learned that Herod, frustrated at not having been able to find the baby he so desperately sought, had ordered the slaying of all male babies two years and younger in or near Bethlehem, and the order had been carried out. And then Mary wept bitterly, saying, "I think of Rebecca and her joy in her son, Isaiah, who is no more." She moved from side to side, keening, her own child pressed against her heart.

CHAPTER THIRTEEN

...

Nazareth

AUGUST, A.D. 9

Joseph

Joseph and Jesus washed for dinner outside the house. The younger children watched, the two little girls, Anna and Lydia, jumping up and down and clapping their hands. They were eager for Joseph's attention, and he was eager to give it to them. They liked when he unfastened the thongs of his leather belt, unhitching his wooden mallet and iron chisel. Each evening they fought playfully about who would have the privilege of putting his tools away in the workshop. Performing this task, they imitated Joseph's care and attentiveness, and it made him proud that his characteristics were so clearly in them. Anna and Lydia both took pride in being able to name these and other tools: the file and dowel pin, the auger and plane. He was more accommodating of his daughters' inquisitiveness and love of learning than he had been of his wife's: such were the softening and conciliatory effects of marriage and children. He did not protest his daughters' endless questions about things that did not properly concern them; rather, he took pride in their quick and eager minds. They would come with ease to their natural roles of wives and mothers, he was sure, for they demonstrated the same eagerness to learn with Mary when she taught them bread making and weaving, laundry and child care.

Joseph's body hurt him this evening. He ascribed the aching in his joints to the hard labor he and Jesus had performed on an unusually hot day. Hauling stone in such heat had taken a toll, as had cutting wood. Even mixing mortar had been difficult for him today. And his problems with digestion were not going away—often, his belly pained him.

He was not the young man he used to

be. Soon he and Jesus would change roles and he would be his son's helpmate. Would that Jesus shared the enthusiam his daughters had for the trade! But Jesus was an unusual child, given to long periods of silence and seclusion. Once, at planting time, as Jesus stared at the seeds that lay in his hand rather than sowing them, Joseph had come to stand beside him. He had lain his hand on Jesus' shoulder and asked gently, "What is it you see, my son, that so captures your attention?"

"God," Jesus had said, still focused on the seeds. Then he had looked up and repeated softly, "God," and there was in his tone not so much explanation as entreaty. He is indeed his mother's son, Joseph had thought, remembering the way that, early in their courtship, Mary had talked to him about evidence of the Almighty in nature, indeed in everything around them.

Jesus finished washing first and went into the house. There, Joseph knew, he would talk to his mother in private. Jesus and Mary had a close relationship, what seemed at times an exclusionary one, even, but Joseph did not mind. Jesus had since birth endured certain hardships—there were still those who talked behind their hands when he passed, and he was known pointedly as "Mary's son." Jesus took solace from Joseph's quiet and steady claim to him as a son, but he seemed to need his talks with his mother—they thought in like ways.

Years after Jesus' birth, Mary still insisted that he was divine, that it was the angel's visit alone that accounted for his conception. Joseph upheld her reputation despite his ongoing doubt. He supposed he would need his own miracle to convert his belief to hers!

But in the end, Joseph had his own way of looking at Jesus. What was it that made a man? Was it the seed alone? Was all that a man would become present at—or before—his birth? Surely not. Surely Jesus was shaped by Joseph even as were his other children.

Yet Joseph had to admit there was something exceptional about their firstborn; Mary was right in this. The extraordinary circumstances surrounding his birth. The mysterious nature of his personality, his protracted periods of intense contemplation. The way he often seemed unreachable, even as he stood directly before a person. He was oddly restless, too, as Mary had been. But perhaps he would outgrow this, for Mary was restless no longer. Now she reveled in her life as a normal Nazarene woman. She met Yola and Naomi in the courtyard every morning, and as they attended to their chores they talked with great pleasure. Joseph had once come upon them so seized by laughter they could not speak, but only waved their hands helplessly about when asked the reason for their hilarity.

Mary had told Joseph that much of the women's time was spent talking about their families, and she had shared with him what Naomi had said about Jesus: "She said I must make him more like other children."

"Ah," Joseph had said. He agreed wholeheartedly with Naomi, but he had learned over the years to tread lightly with Mary, that he did not force her to defend herself. "And how did you reply?"

"I replied that I shall encourage even more his independence and free spirit. For one of my greatest joys is to argue with Naomi, who believes always that her opinion is the irrefutable truth."

"Mary—" he had begun.

And she had sighed and said, "I know, my husband."

For her part, Mary seemed to have learned the value of Joseph's conservative point of view. He had explained over and over to her the necessity of adherence to tradition, for without it they would lose their identity. He had invoked the sacred covenant it was their obligation to honor: if they lived in accordance with God's commandments and prohibitions, he would intervene in human affairs and drive the Romans from Israel, as justice called for. "What bitterness Judas Maccabaeus would taste if he knew of the Roman rule, and of those who have turned their back on the laws of our patriarchs to cooperate with the Romans!" Joseph had told Mary. He had told her also of his strong belief that each person was called to the test each day, that there was an ongoing war inside the self, and the challenge was to always honor what was right. What he did not speak of was something he believed Mary knew anyway: that he had gone against deeply held principles in marrying her when she was with a child not his own. Moreover, he had never regretted it, which he worried was an even greater sin. His love for Mary enriched and enlivened him, gave his life structure and purpose and limitless joy. Also, it tormented him.

Now he came into the house and sat at the large table, and Mary ladled out the soup she had made. There was also dried beef over which Josus and Judas would surely fight—each liked it exceedingly well. Their younger sons, Simon and James, were quiet and polite but too thin. Tonight Joseph would offer the beef to them first.

The younger sons asked Joseph and Jesus many questions about their work that day—they had finished a project in Sepphoris. After such accomplishments, they always enjoyed a feast. Today it had been roasted meat and vegetables on flatbread and a basket of apricots and almonds. After they detailed the delicious food they had enjoyed—even as they were enjoying the delicious food!—they talked about how fine the building looked. "Better than all the buildings that surround it," Jesus said, and looked across the table for his father's agreement.

"Better by far," Joseph said, smiling.

That night Mary and Joseph allowed their

children to sleep on the roof, so long as the smallest three were kept to the far inside. Even Jesus had joined them, a rarity—usually, if he slept outside, it was in the fields, by himself.

"Our Jesus seeks company this night," Joseph said as he lay on his pallet beside Mary. "Yet he must endeavor to be with others more often; he is too much alone. Even working beside me, he often seems alone."

"Though he labors now as your assistant, his real work is yet to come," Mary said. "Perhaps it is thoughts of this that so occupy him."

Joseph scoffed. "His real work, you say! As when he remained behind at the temple when last we journeyed to Jerusalem for Passover? And we were so frightened until we found him? You especially, my wife! And then, upon finding him, to have him tell us that he was 'about his father's work'!"

"Do you recall as well that the teachers were impressed with him?" Mary asked.

Joseph said nothing.

"That they said—"

"I remember," Joseph said. "Yet he is still a child and not yet a man. He is only beginning to learn what he must to make his way in the world."

"You are teaching him well," Mary said. "For it is from you he has learned that the greatest of things is love. That the skill most valuable is belief in oneself. That inside the soul is something longing to speak, if only we will listen."

Joseph laughed. "And it was you who taught me that!"

"It is not so," Mary said. "I fear we have become so close we know not where one ends and the other begins! But I assure you, our children and I, too, have learned much from you. It is you who has made me content with my life, you who has brought such peace to my heart. Do you still not know how I admire you?"

"Even though I have performed no miracles?" Joseph liked to tease Mary about what she called Jesus' "miracles": The easing of a pain in Mary's back after he had touched it. The way, when he was six and was sent to the well for water, he was jostled and dropped the clay pitcher, breaking it, but brought home water anyway, carrying it in a thin shirt, through which, by all rights, it should have leaked out. Joseph had no explanation for these things, but he balked against calling them miracles.

"Jesus longs for your love and respect," Mary said quietly.

"I do love him," Joseph said. "As I love all my children. As I love their beautiful mother." He leaned over and kissed her forehead, her eyes, and her mouth. Then he put his hand to the side of her face and smiled at her. He kissed her collarbone and felt her relax against him. Other men complained of their wives' attempts at rejection, but Mary never denied him. Never mind that it was becoming difficult to care for so large a family at a time when work for Joseph was less than it ever had been. Never mind that yet another mouth to feed and small body to clothe would make things more difficult still, even with Jesus beginning to contribute to the family. Since the first night in Egypt when Joseph had at last known Mary, she had seemed to relish his attentions, and she welcomed each new child with joy.

But now he pulled suddenly away from her.

"Joseph?" There was alarm in her voice.

He wanted to reassure her but could not

speak. He winced, holding his hand to his abdomen. Finally, "It must be the apricots," he said. "Perhaps they were not ripe."

"Shall I prepare anemones for you?"

He gasped and softly cried out. After a moment, he took her hand and kissed it. "Thank you, but there is no need." Anemones did not help his pain any longer, nor did the galangal Mary gave him to relieve his nausea. "I apologize, my dear wife. Stay here and take your rest; I shall walk for a time in the night air. In the morning, I shall be greatly improved, I am sure."

"If you are going outside, I shall come with you."

He smiled at her. "As you wish." He leaned in closer. "We shall have an *adventure*." But he had come to relish the idea of such things, too.

He rose to his knees, then abruptly sat down. "Though it is probably unwise to walk when it is so late. We should take our rest." He lay down, bit at his lower lip, and clenched his fists. The *pain*!

Mary lay close to him. He could feel her praying, and he closed his eyes and prayed with her.

CHAPTER FOURTEEN

. . .

Nazareth

SEPTEMBER, A.D. 9

Mary

He moans, the smallest of sounds, and she draws him closer. He looks up at her, searching her face. "I fear you will forget me."

"Joseph. You are my beloved. You run in my veins."

"Who will care for you now?"

"I shall be cared for by caring for our children."

He grimaces, then speaks with soft authority. "You must teach them humility. And groom them for their proper roles. Instill in them the need to honor our traditions, for without them—"

"Do not trouble yourself, my husband, do you not understand that I already know what you will ask of me? And that I will gladly do all of it?"

Joseph shivers and closes his eyes. When he opens them, Mary sees that a certain dullness has come into them. He is dying, then; the time has come. She feels a rush of great pain, but overcomes it by looking out at the land and stilling herself at the center. Later will be the time for her private sorrow; now she must take care of him. She looks down at her husband and smiles.

"I cannot help but worry about Jesus," Joseph says. "I have loved him well, and endured much for his sake, as you have also."

"God knows!" Mary answers. "And I know also that although you love all your children, it is Jesus who is closest to your heart."

He smiles wanly. "Only because of my circumstances do I allow you to say such a thing."

"Is it not true?" she asks.

"I shall ask you now for the truth, Mary. Will you finally tell me?"

"I have told you the truth, Joseph, and I will tell you yet again. On that day, the Holy Spirit—"

"A Roman soldier," Joseph says.

Mary stops breathing. "What do you say?"

"It was a Roman soldier. Naomi saw you with him, and bound me never to reveal to you what she told me. But I must now betray her confidence in order that I at last come to—"

"It is untrue."

"Naomi saw you!"

"Oh, Joseph. I know it is easier to believe a lie that makes sense than a truth you cannot understand. But I tell you it was an angel who gave me the message, and the Holy Spirit who planted the seed. Why have you struggled so long with this when you yourself have had such visions? For an angel told you to take me unto you as your wife. An angel bid you move your family to Egypt, then to Jerusalem, and finally back to Nazareth!"

He raises his shoulders, grown thin unto sharpness by his illness. "I had dreams, it is true. But I saw no angels."

"But, Joseph, you—"

"I ask you again, as I asked you once so long ago: How do we know angels are not a trick of the mind? Or too much drink? Too much sorrow turned to too much hope? As for what you and your mother and Elizabeth saw, women always embroider and embellish the truth. They are natural storytellers. It is part of their nature and part of their charm. But are we to believe all they say? At this time for confessions, I confess my great doubt to you."

She presses her hand to her breast, astonished. "But…*you*! You who are so true to your traditions, to the dictums of your faith! You who are the most religious man in the village!"

He laughs, one small sound. "It is ironic, I admit. You, who speak never of your faith, have more than I, who speak regularly of it. But I cannot deny any longer what lies deepest in my heart." He sighs. "I do not believe in angels. Or miracles."

"Would that I had the words to convince you of the truth of these things!"

He smiles ruefully. "I am afraid it is too late for that."

"Joseph. That an angel did not come to you does not make false him coming to another. When I spit out the rotten fig, is it you detesting the taste? As for miracles, it is difficult to acknowledge them, it is true. Yet it is through acceptance of such revelations that we come to our true spiritual natures. In truth, you have witnessed miracles all your life!"

He smiles. "When?"

"Always! For miracles are everywhere around us. Sometimes they are small and common: The curl of a child's ear. The ripening of grapes on the vine. The stretching of a rainbow over the valley in which we live. Sometimes they are larger: That we have inside ourselves the capacity to feel the music we hear. That our people survive!

"And also I admit there are miracles that defy comprehension: my own virgin childbirth. I know how difficult it is to contemplate, how the mind rebels against it. Yet I tell you again that it, too, was a miracle. What have I to gain by being false to you as you lay dying? What terrible retribution do I invite by doing such a thing? What kind of queer pleasure do I hope to find?"

Now, as he looks at her, the faintest of hopes.

"And Joseph, there are miracles you yourself have wrought."

"I!"

"Yes, you. Shall I recount them?"

"First cover me, Mary, for I grow cold."

Her heart in her throat, she removes her shawl and lays it over him. Then she says, "Have you not covered me with your own blanket of a cold winter's night and in summertime given me water that was yours to drink?"

He nods, his eyes shining with tears.

"By this and by countless other acts, you, an earthbound man, have made his wife certain she lives with him in heaven. Thereby do I provide you with evidence for one of your miracles. And there are many more: That a heart so damaged as yours could heal to hold such love, not only for me but for seven children, all of whom are certain of being your special favorite. That despite our often desperate circumstances, not once has any of us been made to want—for you have held your family always in your mind and in your heart, and by your hand provided for us. You have shown by your life's example what love and forgiveness can transcend. These are examples enough for me. Are they not enough for you, as well?"

". . . Perhaps."

"Perhaps?!"

He shakes his head. "Even on my deathbed, you will argue with me." He takes her hand, and she is careful not to react to the weakness with which he holds it. "You speak so lovingly of my caring for my family. But I have failed, for I have nothing to leave them."

"Nothing to leave them! Nothing but ideals of honor and of courage, of integrity and forbearance! Of steadfastness and loyalty! Nothing but those things without which nothing else matters!"

"Ah, Mary. Since the first time I saw you under the table at the wedding, where you most beguilingly bumped your head, I have loved only you—with my body, my mind, and my soul. I shall wait in joyful anticipation for you to be once more beside me. But first, live long and well, that you may care for our children and enjoy this life so rich with the miracles you have described." Slowly, he rises to his elbows and makes his expression stern. "I order this, my wife!"

"And I shall, as ever, obey."

He lies down again, takes her hand, and kisses her fingers. "My beauty. From where did you come?"

"I was spun of a spider's web."

"It is you who are my miracle." He starts to say more but then suddenly turns away from her to stare at something in the darkness. "Look, Mary! Who draws nigh?"

She can make out nothing. "What is it, Joseph?"

His face is rapt, and he points with a trembling hand. "See now, an angel comes! Do you see him? Such terrible beauty; do you see how his countenance shines? Oh, I see now that you and the others have spoken the truth, for I see him plainly. But look, he draws near! I am afraid!"

She speaks quietly to him. "Then I shall hold you close to me and wait with you for his warmth to surround and transport you." She reaches under his knees and shoulders and draws him awkwardly to her. He leans into her, trembling, staring out at the space before them. And then he stills. Slowly, he reaches out an arm. He smiles, and there is in it an eagerness: a child looking with happy anticipation around the corner. And then he moves no more.

She bows her head, then lifts it to stare out at the horizon, where a hint of red signals the rising sun. She pulls Joseph closer to her and rocks him. Always at dawn, as well as before going to bed, he has recited the Shema, and she says it now for him:

"Sh'ma Yisrael Adonai Elohaynu Adonai Echad," she begins, softly. *Hear, Israel, the Lord is our God, the Lord is One.* Then, more surely, she continues:

*Blessed be the name of his glorious
    kingdom forever and ever.
And you shall love the Lord your God
    with all your heart and with all your
    soul and with all your might.
And these words that I command you
    today shall be in your heart.
And you shall teach them diligently to
    your children, and you shall speak of
    them when you sit at home, and
    when you walk along the way, and
    when you lie down and when you
    rise up.
And you shall bind them as a sign on
    your hand, and they shall be for
    frontlets between your eyes.
And you shall write them on the door-*

*posts of your house and on your
gates.*
*And it shall come to pass if you surely
listen to the commandments that I
command you today, to love the Lord
your God, and to serve him with all
your heart and all your soul,*
*That I will give rain to your land, the
early and the late rains,*
*That you may gather in your grain, your
wine, and your oil.*
*And I will give grass in your fields for
your cattle, and you will eat and you
will be satisfied.*

She stops speaking, and rocks from side
to side, her head bent to her husband's.
What does she wish for now? That the
whole world could know of this unassuming
man's devotion, and all that it has provided.
But they are from a simple village whose in-
habitants are looked down upon and
scorned. All she can do for him is give him
a proper burial, which she will do. She will
have her sons carry his body down from the
roof and lay him on his pallet. She will wash
him and anoint him and wrap him in flax,

and then he will be buried, and all the village will mourn him.

She will visit his grave often. She will speak to him of their seven children, and of herself, and of all the people, living and dead, whom they have known. She will speak of the coming of the seasons, of the births and the deaths in their town. She will speak of the way that love endures, for she knows beyond doubt that their love will. But most often she will speak to him of Jesus, whom he so regretted, yet so loved.

It will pain all of her children to learn of Joseph's passing, but especially Jesus, because of his extraordinary sensitivity. It comes to Mary that he already knows his father has died, that he lies on his pallet below them waiting for his mother to confirm what has already come to his heart.

The night wind picks up her hair and blows it wild about her face. She tucks it behind her ears and bends down to kiss her husband's forehead, his eyelids, his mouth. Then she pulls herself gently from Joseph and goes down the stairs to Jesus. It is to him she must now attend.

ABOUT THE AUTHOR

Elizabeth Berg is the author of fifteen novels, including the *New York Times* bestsellers *The Art of Mending, Say When, True to Form, Never Change,* and *Open House,* which was an Oprah's Book Club selection in 2000. *Durable Goods* and *Joy School* were selected as ALA Best Books of the Year, and *Talk Before Sleep* was short-listed for the ABBY Award in 1996. The winner of the 1997 New England Booksellers Award for her work, she is also the author of the nonfiction work *Escaping into the Open: The Art of Writing True*. She lives in Chicago.